George Ade

Pink Marsh

A Story of the Streets and Town

George Ade

Pink Marsh
A Story of the Streets and Town

ISBN/EAN: 9783337400255

Printed in Europe, USA, Canada, Australia, Japan

Cover: Foto ©Andreas Hilbeck / pixelio.de

More available books at **www.hansebooks.com**

PINK MARSH

A Story of the Streets and Town

BY

GEORGE ADE
AUTHOR OF "ARTIE"

PICTURES BY

JOHN T. McCUTCHEON

HERBERT S. STONE & CO.
CHICAGO & NEW YORK
1897

THIS STORY IS REWRITTEN FROM A
SERIES OF SKETCHES WHICH FIRST
APPEARED IN THE CHICAGO RECORD

On Spending a Million Dollars

He happened into the place one afternoon in the late autumn. They met by
chance—the usual way. If he had shaved
himself that morning, as he should have
done, he never would have met Pink.
Perhaps Fate issued a sub-decree.

That afternoon as he moved through
the weaving crowd toward the corner
where his trolley-car stopped for him, he
felt of his face and found it stubbled. The
shop opened invitingly at the bottom of a
white stairway. Most of the barber-shops
in Chicago are underground. He descended to the shop and sat in the first
chair. When he had been tilted back he
closed his eyes so as to keep away the
horrors of a ceiling-design. The conver-

sation, which had ceased when he entered, was then taken up again.

"I know, but s'pose you *did* find a million dollars. Would n't you keep it?'"

"That depends."

"Don' ask me, Misteh Adams. I would n' keep no million dollahs faw minute, would·I? They 'd have to chlo'fohm me to get 'at money 'way f'om me."

"Yes, but then if you give it back to the man that owned it he might give you as much as twenty thousand dollars."

"Who would? My goodness, misteh white man bahbch, people don' get no million dollahs now'days by givin' 'way money. No, seh! Huh-uh! It 's 'bout fo' to one 'at any man 's got as much as million dollahs ain't goin' 'o open up. Chances is he 'd give you 'bout fo' dollahs."

"Yes, but what good would this money do you? If you went to throwin' a million dollars around do n't you s'pose the police 'd be onto you? They 'd be lookin' for the man that found the money."

" You could n't have that money ten minutes without flashin' it."

" Look heah, I fool you. Do you reckon I 'd spend 'at money right away ? No, seh! I 'd wait 'bout six months an' 'en I 'd jus' begin lettin' go little at time. I 'd pull big, elegant hundehd out o' my cloze an' some one say, ' Boy, wheah you get 'at green stuff?' I say I win it on 'e faw-'eign book. I 'd p'ten' to be gamblin', un'e'stand ? I 'd go to New Yawk o' some othah place an' bring roll back an' tell 'em I win it."

" What are you givin' us? As soon as you got hold of that stuff you 'd go down and buy all the blue clothes on Clark street."

" Then he 'd get gay an' tell that Twenty-fourth Street girl all about it an' she 'd tell somebody else an' they 'd have him in the booby-hatch in about two hours."

At this there was general laughter, and the one who had been consigned to the " booby-hatch" laughed hoarsely after the others had quieted.

" No, seh; I guess I wouldn' betteh stay 'roun' 'iss town," he said. " I get me one of 'em p'ivate Pullman cahs an' go travelin' 'roun' 'e country. I wouldn' do thing—'bout fo' cullud boys to wait on me. 'Heah, boy, open 'notheh box of 'em cigahs an' put two mo' bottles on ice.' My goodness! Get into new town, wave my han" jus' like 'at—up come caih'age. Get in, you know, drive 'roun' mos' p'ominent thuhfaihs—"

" What's that last word ? "

" He do n't know. He heard somebody out on Armour Avenue say that."

" I 'd be strong 'ith 'em cullud guhls too. My goodness, Miss Ruth, who 's 'at new gemman 'ith all 'em di'mon's an' rubies. Yes, seh, I 'd have 'em settin' traps faw me! Could n't keep 'em away nohow."

" I guess you 've had some trouble already keepin' away that one you owe the laundry bill to."

" Hush! man!" and he laughed again. The barber at work had to poise his razor until he could control himself, while the man in the chair smiled through the lather.

" Le' me tell you—I 'd pay 'at woman what I owe 'uh an' give huh hundehd dollah bill, an' 'en I 'd neveh speak to huh agen. She eveh come up to me I say, ' Woman, I can't place you; go back to yo' own kind o' people.' "

" O, you 'd get proud, would you? I do n't s'pose you 'd speak to any of us, would you."

" I might 'membah seein' you somewheahs, but I sutny wouldn' know you ve'y well. I 'd be too busy countin' money to fool my time on bahbehs. C'ose

I'd let you have dollah o' two, but you would n' see me minglin' 'ith pooh men. You want to see me, you send in yo' cahd by 'at cullud boy, an' I look it oveh an' say, 'Adams? Adams? Seems to me I see 'at name somewheahs. Tell 'im to wipe his feet an' come in.'"

"Yes, an' then you'd go in an' find him at a gold table, with a watermelon on one side of him and a fried chicken on the other."

"That ain' no bad guess, mistah! You can't tell, neetheh—might be po'teh-house steak 'ith onions. I'd jus' be settin' theah, stahvin' to death! You know I have all 'ese cullud men to wait on me— one to brush my cloze, one to shine my shoes, 'notheh to wait on 'e table, an' I'd have one cullud boy 'ith nothin' to do 'cept think o' what I want to eat. 'Heah boy, what you goin' 'o gi' me f' sup-peh?' 'Well,' he say, 'I got a little po'teh-house—an' quail, an' pohk-chops

—le 's see, sweet potatoes, ice-cream, chahlum-rushe—"

" Look out there! "

" O, got to have some of 'at stuff—cla'et, an' fancy cakes an' champagne."

" What are you talkin' about? You wuz n't built to stand anything better 'n gin."

" See heah, misteh, when I 'uz waitin' on 'e table faw big banq'et an' gemman leave some of 'at champagne—I s'pose I took 'at wine an' th'owed it away, did n' I? Yes, seh, I used to get it befo' 'em little beads stop jumpin'."

Then there was a shuffle of feet, for some one had come down the stairway. A gruff voice asked, " Say, can you fix up these tans for me in a hurry? "

" Yes, sch, 'at's sutny jus' what I can do."

" While you 're rubbin' out that ten-cent piece you can think over some more ways to spend that million."

"—When he gets it."

" The most money he ever had at one time was sixteen dollars. That was when he got on that seven-to-one shot. He did n't work for three days."

There was a sound of suppressed laughter in the corner. The man who had chanced into the place unfolded himself from the chair and saw the colored boy at work, throbbing with exertion.

" Brush!" shouted the barber, but the customer did not wait for the ceremonial. He ran for his car, and all the way home he leaned back in a warm reverie and helped the boy spend the million.

"MISTEH ADAMS"

On Being Virtuous in Order to be Happy

Without confessing to himself that he remembered the first visit, he went to the shop one morning to have his shoes cleaned. The first conversation was the mere commonplace which passes between the employer and the employed. It related to the kind of polish to be used. Pink saw before him only a pair of shoes. He little suspected—but there is no need of anticipating.

The customer sat in an arm-chair which was placed on top of a box-like rostrum. The box and the chair were studded with brass tacks and other metal ornaments. They would have served as a Congo throne. William Pinckney

Marsh usually had the market page of yesterday's paper tucked under the chair cushion.

Pink's shirt was a black and white study of trellises, with vines climbing up them.

The vest was double-breasted, and had been once polka-dot silk, but now the dots were mostly blurred away and the pockets had begun to ravel.

His trousers were black and brown check, worn thin at the knees and ragged at the bottom.

The shoes were extremely pointed, two sizes too large, cracked across the top and protuberant at the heel.

When Pink was dressed for the street he wore also a double-breasted coat tightly buttoned, a spreading blue necktie that had been handled once or twice too often, a high white collar and a light brown hat with a high crown. Pink improved as you studied him from the ground upward.

His apparel might have been judged as follows :

Shoes—Utterly disreputable.

Trousers—Shabby.

Coat—Badly worn.

Necktie—Showy.

Collar—Splendid.

Hat—Magnificent.

What need to tell of the coal-black face, the broad-flanged nose, the elastic mouth opening on teeth of pearly whiteness, and the close growth of kinky hair?

A song of passing popularity tells that all members of the Ethiopian division "look alike." Pink was one of a thousand—that is, so far as mere appearance was concerned.

When it came to a consideration of the higher being—the sure-enough ego—Pink was different. He saw things from his own standpoint, and there was room for no one else on his pedestal.

On this first morning he came to his

task languidly, and even lazily. After some sleepy preparations, he drew a heavy sigh and attacked the shoes fiercely. It will never be known whether Pink was a tired mortal driven to work, or an industrious mortal who had to restrain himself by certain affectations.

He was at his best when he walked. He allowed his feet to shuffle so that the movement was a sort of slow dance-step.

He seemed to be keeping time to music which only the rapt and colored soul may hear.

The morning customer learned in two or three visits that the barbers liked Pink and pitied him. They were men who had given much study to public questions. Pink came in on their back-and-forth discussions. He pieced in observations which amused them, and also convinced them that Pink lacked seriousness of purpose. They regarded him as a sort of court jester. Sometimes they patronized

PART OF THE MORNING PAPER

him half in kindness, but they never forgot
that there was a social chasm between a
barber and a " brush."

Perhaps Pink did not fully understand the significance of their manner
toward him, or he would have been cast
down in spirit. As it was, the humility
which he made his main stock in trade,
was merely an outward pretense.

The morning customer learned this on
the occasion of his third visit, up to which
time the conversation had been along the
lines of rather strict formality. At the
second visit he crossed Pink's palm
with silver, so that when he came the third
time he saw a mellow smile in the corner.
The barbers were talking on the relations
of Church and State that morning.

The morning customer appeared to
be amiable and receptive when Pink
looked up at him.

" Listen at 'em toss 'at lang'age. Ain't
they wahm ? If you wan 'o know any-

thing, you jus' come to 'em boys an' ask. If 'ey do n' know, no use to look in 'em books. It ain't theah—could n' be."

" They 're up on everything, eh ? "

" Oh-h-h, wise — wise boys. Cong'ess could n' tell 'em boys nothin' 'bout how to do it. No, seh, 'em rascals is sutny good."

Pink folded the drying-cloth and went at the shoe again, singing softly :

    ''Misteh Johnson, tuhn me loose,
      Got no money but good es-cuse;
      O, Misteh Johnson, I wis't you would.
      Oh-h-h — ''

" A new song? " asked the morning customer.

" Ain' it wahm? "

" Who 's Mister Johnson? "

" Misteh Johnson, he 's a coppeh. He come in on a small game o' craps, an' 'at 's what 'at cullud fellow 's singin' to him at 'e box."

" Does that song relate to one of your own experiences ? "

" No, seh — me ? I nevah got 'rested
— faw rollin' craps — no, seh."

" What was it you got arrested for ? "

" Who said I got 'rested ? "

" O, you never were arrested, eh ? "

Pink's elastic mouth widened, and he
laughed so that he had to stop work.

" Look heah, man, who 's been tellin'
you 'bout me ? "

" O, you have been arrested ? "

" I got 'uh once, but it wuz n' no craps,
no, seh."

" Chickens ? "

" W'y, say, look heah, misteh, somebody been paintin' me bad to you. No,
seh, 'ey done it to me faw what 'at judge
called disohdehly."

" How about it? Were you disorderly? "

" Them 'at could 'membeh what happened give in bad tes'imony. I had to dig
up ol' six dollahs to keep out of 'at big
black wagon. No, seh, I do n' wan' no
mo'."

" You 'd been drinking, had n't you ? "

" Yes, seh, 'at 's what made me dange'ous — wuz 'at oil o' distuhb'ance. I don' wan' no mo' to do 'ith 'em coppehs an' blue wagons an' judges. Cullud man sutny can't beat 'at game."

" That 's right," said the morning customer. 'Be virtuous, and you will be happy.'"

" What is 'at 'spression ? Say it oveh. Be — "

" ' Be virtuous, and you will be happy.'"

" O, I guess some one-ahm man wrote 'at ! 'Be vuhchus, an' you will suahly be happy !' My goodness ! I guess 'at 's pooh lang'age ! I sutny will use 'at on 'em Deahbohn Street rascals. Yes, seh, I 'll jus' brush you a few an' you sutny will be all right. Any time, Misteh, you goin' 'o th'ow 'at ovehcoat away, jus' th'ow it at me. No clothin' stoah eveh see 'at coat 'cept when you walk past. Ten — yes, seh — 'at 's 'e

"MISTEH CLIFFO'D"

propeh 'mount.   Good day, seh.   Misteh,
have I got 'at?   Be vuhchus, an' you
will sutny be happy.   Yes, seh — yo 's
truly — good day, seh."

On the Proper Observance of Christmas

The holiday season was at hand the next time the morning customer went to the shop. As he climbed into the chair he saw on the wall, within easy reach, a pasteboard box capped with a sprig of green. In the side of the box was a slit large enough to receive a silver dollar. Below it were the words: " Merry Xmas. Remeber the porter."

" What does that mean — ' Merry Xmas ' ? " asked the customer.

Pink shook his head slowly. " You know mighty well what 'at means, misteh. If I on'y had yo' ej'cation I would n' be whippin' flannel oveh no man's shoes."

" I do n't see what education has to do

"MY GOODNESS!"

with it. What is it, anyway — that
' Merry Xmas ' ? "

" Misteh Cliffo'd, on 'e secon' chaih,
made it faw me. He says 'at 's ' Me'y
Ch'is'mas.' "

" That 's a funny way to spell Christmas. What does the rest of it mean
there — about remembering the porter ? "

" My goodness, misteh, you ain' goin'
'o fo'ce me to come right out an' ask faw
it, ah you ? "

" Ask for what ? "

Pink emitted a series of heaving
sounds to indicate that he was amused.

" Mr. Clifford did a very fine job there,"
observed the customer.

" Who, Misteh Cliffo'd ? He can do
mos' anything. He 's got watch-chain
made out o' real haih, he made himself."

" He must be a versatile genius."

" I guess he — say, misteh, 'at wuz a
wahm piece o' talk. What was 'at you
say — he — "

" I say he must be a versatile genius."

" A vussitle gemyus — genimus."

" Genius — versatile genius."

" Vussitle gen'us — 'at 's lolly-cooleh. If I on'y had a few like 'at I 'd keep 'em ketchin' theah breaths, suah. What 's 'e def'mition ? "

" That means a man of varied accomplishments."

Pink worked a few minutes and allowed the definition to percolate. Then he observed with a sigh : " I could n' ketch 'em boys ; not 'ith a laddeh. Too high."

The barber at chair No. 1 shouted " Brush ! " and Pink shuffled away to attend to a thin man with a powdered complexion and gummy hair.

First he brushed the thin man, front and back, becoming more earnest in his efforts just as the man received a handful of small change. Pink held the overcoat, and after the thin man had worked into it, he reached under for the inside coat and pulled it down so violently that the thin man was bowed backward. While Pink was brushing the overcoat the thin man walked over and took his hat from the hook.

But he was not to escape so easily. Pink gently pulled the hat away from him and went in search of the small brush. He stood in front of the thin customer, and, holding the hat gingerly in the left hand, brushed it carefully, at the same time blowing off imaginary specks of dust.

While the thin man was waiting for his hat he casually put his right hand into the trousers pocket. Pink stopped brushing and scratched at an invisible spot or stain of some sort on the sleeve of the overcoat.

"Shine?" he inquired softly.

"Nope."

He continued to brush the hat.

The thin man withdrew his hand from the pocket. Pink turned the hat around right side forward and presented it to the customer with a bow. The customer's right hand moved forward a few inches, but Pink's broad palm met it more than half-way. The nickel passed.

"Thank you, seh," said Pink in a reverential whisper. The thin man started toward the door. Pink seized the long whisk-broom and pursued him, hitting him between the shoulder-blades. As the man passed out Pink got in one final blow on the coat-tails.

"You 're doing well to-day," observed the morning customer when Pink had returned to his place in the corner.

Pink dropped the nickel to the floor, as if by accident. Then he picked it up, turned it over and put it in his mouth.

"Money layin' all 'roun' heah to-day," he said, rattling the coin against his teeth.

"You can buy a loaf of bread with that," suggested the customer.

"You betteh make anothah guess on what I 'm goin' 'o do 'ith any nicks I get

hold of 'ese days. Bread 's faw pooh people. I 'm goin' 'o eat chidlin's, roas' pig,
cawnpone, che'y pie, mash' tuhnips an'
—le' me see—"

" You 'll be lucky to get snowballs,"
interrupted the barber known as ' Misteh
Adams,' who had strolled over to the
corner to watch the boy at work.

" Don' lose no sleep 'bout me," re-
torted Pink. " I may be baihfoot an'
need mo' undeh-cloze, but I sutny will
have my chidlin's on Ch'is'mas, an' any
man 'at thinks diff'ent wants to make a
new guess, suah. If 'at ol' box up on 'e
wall uses me good I 'll be a wahm baby
'iss Ch'is'mas—yes, seh, I 'll eat oystehs
'ith my true love."

" How are you and that girl gettin'
along now?" asked Mr. Adams, with a
palpable wink at the morning customer.

" I do n' know nothin' 'bout no guhl,"
replied Pink with a sly grin. " No, seh,
Misteh Adams, I got no money to waste

on no piece o' calico. I'm jus' wantin'
to feed myse'f 'iss Ch'is'mas. No use
talkin'! You know what 'at col' wind
say when it comes zoo-in an' whistlin'
roun' 'e cohneh. It say, ' Boy, wheah's
all 'at money you spent faw ice-cream an'
neckties las' summeh ?"

"Mistah Adams" walked away and
Pink said, in a low tone: "You do n' ketch
me tellin' any white bahbeh 'bout 'at
lady."

"Have n't you got any money for
Christmas ?" asked the morning customer.

"No, seh, I got to get someping out of
'at box."

"You ought to be able to save a little
money."

"Down theah wheah I live, misteh, it
ain' safe f' man to have no money. If
'em tough cullud boys think you' savin'
yo' coin 'ey jus' stop you at night an'
count it faw you. Yes, seh, an' when
'ey get th'ough countin' it, 'em boys han'

back to you what 'ey do n' need. If anybody goin' 'o spen' my money I want to
spend it myse'f."

" Why do n't you put it in the bank ? "

" Yes, seh, I 'm goin' 'o put some in 'e
bank next yeah."

" Well, you want to bear well in mind
that procrastination is the thief of time."

" Le' go, man ! ' At 's sutny 'e hottes'
thing you handed me yet. Pocazzumala-
shum — prasticanashum — chenashalum—
no, seh, thea h's one too good faw me. No,
seh, don' try to gi' me 'at one. It keep me
busy jus' foldin' kinks out of 'at boy.

" Why, that 's very simple—procrastination. It means the habit of postponing
action, putting off until to-morrow, as it
were."

" 'At 's all right what 'at means, misteh.
I ain' strong enough to swing 'at kind—
pocrastumalation—timination—"

" Procrastination."

" No, seh, do n' try it, I can't use 'at

boy. 'Ey would n' stan' faw nothin'
like 'at on Deahbohn Street. You keep
'at one an' use it yo'se'f—proclast-pocras-
um-unn-unn—misteh, you sutny have
wuhds up yo' sleeve 'at is strangehs to
me."

" Procrastination is a good word," said
the morning customer as he slipped a
quarter into the Christmas-box and descended from the high-chair.

" Thank you, seh," repeated Pink, three
times.

" 'Ey 's sutny ve'y few men can use
'em wuhds as you do," said he, as he was
brushing the morning customer. " 'Pras-
tigumation is what steals away yo' time'—
no, seh, do n' tell me no mo'; it 's too
high. Good mawnin'. Yes, seh. Same to
you, misteh. Me'y Ch'is'mas."

On Winning the Affections of a Woman

The morning customer learned by experience that Pink thrived on a diet of long words. He could not determine whether Pink's admiration for these words was real or feigned, and it mattered little so long as the boy pretended to be in ecstasy.

One day, toward the close of the holiday season, the morning customer learned something of Pink's love affairs. This was really the beginning of his term as guide, counselor, and friend.

"Good morning, Pink," he said, as he came in. "I trust you have had your matutinal this morning."

"My goodness, misteh! I might have

27

my pockets full of 'at stuff an' not know it. I ain't had nothin' 'iss mawnin' 'cept breakfas'."

" Got a morning paper ? "

" I got paht o' one heah, misteh," and Pink reached under the chair for it.

" Part of one, eh ? I suppose it 's the page of small ads. You 're the only man I ever knew who bought a newspaper on the installment plan. Why do n't you save up some morning and buy a whole paper — have a little enterprise about you? You want to get a new cushion in this chair too. Do n't you know you have to treat customers well in order to hold trade these days ? "

Pink restrained his mirth and sighed with enjoyment.

" Misteh, you sutny good."

While he was working with the rough brush to remove the dry and encrusted mud, he sung softly :

"A HOT MEMBEH"

" I do n' love a-nobody,
An' nobody loves me.
Yo' afteh my money —
Do n' caih faw me.
I 'm goin'o stay single,
Always-a be free;
I do n' love a-nobody,
An' nobody loves me."

The morning customer folded the paper in his lap and listened to the song.

" Is that your private confession? " he asked.

" How 's 'at, misteh? "

" You do n't love anybody, eh? "

" Co'se, misteh, I 'uz jus' singin' what it says in 'at song."

" O, I see. So you do love somebody, after all? I believe I 've heard something about that girl out there."

" Out wheah, misteh — out wheah? You neveh saw 'at guhl in all yo' life, misteh. What you want to say 'at faw? "

" I did n't say I ever saw her. I said I 'd heard about her."

Pink laughed to himself until his frizzled head bobbed up and down above the shoe. Then he looked up at the morning customer, his eyes big with doubt, and said, " Yo' stringin' me, misteh."

" Certainly not. I was talkin' to some colored boy the other day — I forget his name. I says to him : ' Do you know William Pinckney Marsh ? ' and he says : ' Do you mean Pink Marsh, the fellow that likes chicken so well ? ' "

" Who said 'at, misteh ? Who was 'at cullud rascal 'at tried to make me out chicken-lifteh ? "

" Do n't get excited. Keep right on with your work. He simply said that you liked chicken. He did n't say that you stole chickens."

" I know, misteh, but what is 'at he means by sayin' I like chicken? Do n't you know cullud man say someping like 'at 'bout anotheh an' he gen'ally got to lose a fight? Yes, seh, you say ' chickens' to cullud man, an' 'at means someping."

" Why, you *do* like chicken, do n't you ? "

" How 's 'at ? W'y—mistch, even if I do, do n't all people like chicken ? "

" I suppose they do, but this friend of yours says that you eat more chicken than any other colored fellow on the South Side."

" Who ? Who ? He say 'at, misteh ? Goodness ! Wis't you could 'membeh his name. I think I 'd hahm 'at man if I get him placed. What else he tell you ? "

" Well, he said you had a girl and that another fellow was trying to cut you out."

" Who—Gawge Lippincott ? "

" Yes, that 's the name, George Lippin-cott. This fellow seemed to think that George had a shade the best of it."

" Do n't you neveh believe it, misteh, not faw minute—no, seh. It ain't wrote in no book 'at Gawge Lippincott can do me at no game—no, seh."

" Who's the girl ? "

" Young lady name Miss Lo'ena Jackson."

" Lorena, eh? That's a fancy name? "

" Yes, seh, an' little ol' Miss Lo'ena's hot membeh. She's so wahm you can feel 'e heat on otheh side of 'e street when she goes past. My goodness! I s'pose she's bad to look at. She had me settin' up nights faw 'while."

" Dark ? "

" No, seh, not as dahk as me, but she ain' no blonde, neetheh. I s'pose 'at guhl ain' got no cloze. My goodness! Get on 'at puhl-cullud cloak 'ith all 'em buttons an' staht 'long Deahbohn Street—face at ev'y window, suah."

" Does she reciprocate your affection ? "

" Do n' make me jump faw 'em, mistah. What is 'at—'cip'ocate ? "

" Does she love you ? "

"JENNIE TAYLAH"

" Misteh, I 'm real thing jus' now, but I can't p'omise no finish. I 'm playin' hahd, but if 'at lady eveh calls me—" and Pink once more shook with laughter.

" I do n't understand you."

" I tell you, misteh. When I staht in to win 'at lady Gawge Lippincott 'uz ve'y strong theah. She could n' see me. Gawge got me beat on ej'cation. We be oveh Mis' Willahd's house—ol' Gawge on sofy—'Miss Lo'ena, I 'm afraid 'e weatheh goin' 'o be mo' 'centrical on 'count of 'at atmosphe'cal management,' someping like 'at. She come back jus' as wahm as he wuz. Me, misteh? Jus' settin' theah an' bein' counted out. I wuz n't in 'at cullud society no mo 'n if I 'd been white. When it come to tossin' lang'age ol' Gawge sutny had me skinned. Jus' same, I figgah out what I got to do to get nex' to 'at lady. I know Miss Lo'ena wants wheel—'cuz Jennie Tayloh's got one in

'e same house, an' kin' o' been th'owin'
it into Lo'ena 'bout not bein' in line.
One night I 'uz talkin' to Lo'ena an' I
say, 'What kin' of a wheel is 'at Jennie
Tayloh's got?' an' she say, 'I think,
Misteh Mahsh, it's one 'at huh motheh
bought at secon'-han' stoah.' Knockin','
un'estand? I say, 'Miss Lo'ena, what
kin' o' wheel you like bes',' an' she say
she like 'at Genemvieve wheel. I pull
out my little book an' write someping in
it. I ask huh what size, an' she say,
'Twent'-six,' an' I say 'Twent'-six,' an'
into 'e book, un'estan', misteh? 'Black
saddle o' tan saddle?' an' she say 'Tan.'
Down it goes into 'at book. You jus'
ought to see 'em eyes. 'Misteh Mahsh,
what you puttin' into 'at book?' 'Neveh
you min'. You find out some day.' My
goodness, misteh! I own 'at lady f'om
'at minute. She know mighty well why I
put all 'at in 'e book. Nex' day she goes
an' tells Jennie Tayloh, 'Misteh Mahsh

goin' 'o buy me Genemvieve wheel.' I
s'pose she 's usin' me bad now."

" Well, are you going to get the wheel?"

" W'y, mistch, you ought to know me
betteh 'n 'at. Way things is comin' now
I could n' buy 'at chain 'at goes on 'e
back wheel. I could n' buy 'nough keh'-
sene to fill 'at little lamp 'at hangs on in
front. Lo'ena knows I 'm goin' 'o buy
huh wheel jus' 'e same. Walkin' 'long
otheh evenin' an' I say, ' Miss Lo'ena,
when 's yo' buhthday,' and she tell me,
' Tenth o' Mahch, but what you want
know 'at faw?' an' I say, ' O, 'at 's all
right, neveh mind!' Look heah, man,when
it come tenth o' Mahch and no wagon
backs up theah 'ith a wheel in it—you
know! I 'll be cold wheat-cake, an' no
mistake! She 'll have Gawge Lippincott
back on huh staff, suah 'nough."

" Well, do you think it 's right to trifle
with a young lady's affections in that
manner?"

" Do n't you botheh 'bout 'at lady,
misteh. She ain' nobody's fool. She
eveh get a wheel out o' me she 'd th'ow me
in 'e aih an' staht out to fin' some suckeh
to buy one of 'em bloomeh suits faw huh.
Yes, seh, she's full of 'at ol' con. She
think she got me right now. I tol' huh
'e otheh evenin', ' Lo'ena, I 'd like to go
an' have some oystehs 'iss ev'nin', but 'e
fact is I 'm savin' ev'y cent o' money I
can get hold of.' Well, co'se she knows
what I 'm savin' faw—got to have 'at
wheel by Mahch, no use talkin'. O, I
do n't know ! I s'pose I 'm foolish ! I
neveh seen cullud lady till I met Miss
Lo'ena."

" What do you think will happen when
this girl finds out for certain that you 're
not going to give her a bicycle ? "

" Neveh you mind. I 'll fix 'at all right.
I 'll get mad at huh an' give 'at wheel to
somebody else. I 'll give it to cullud lady
on 'e Nawth Side."

"O, I see. Well, Pink, I did n't think you 'd be guilty of such malfeasance."

"She 'd do me jus' as much 'feasance if she got chance. She 's out afteh 'at new wheel, an' 'at 's why I 'm ol' papa in 'e pahloh now. Befo' I sprung 'at wheel game, Gawge Lippincott had me done easy—had me faded. I kind o' like 'at lady, but she can't neveh get me foolish enough to let go o' no coin ; no, seh."

"How much does a wheel cost ? "

"Goodness, misteh, keep still! What's 'e use ? I s'pose 'at wheel I 'm goin' 'o buy faw Lo'ena cost eighty dollahs. Hush, man ! If I on'y had 'at much I would n' be foolin' 'ith Miss Lo'ena Jackson. I 'd be wahm boy 'ith 'em swell cullud people down towahds Thuhtieth Street—yes, seh, you could n' lose me."

"Well, that 's all right. If you rub those shoes much longer you 'll wear them out. Here is your piece of silver. I have enjoyed very much the story of your amour."

" Deahbohn—not Ahmoh," said Pink.

The morning customer laughed aloud, and Pink laughed sympathetically, without knowing why he did so. He brushed the morning customer out to the stairway.

On War With England

The morning customer was permitted to see the photograph of Miss Lorena Jackson. He looked at it with evident interest and said, " Stylish, is n't she ? "

" Who ? 'At guhl ? High - steppeh. She 's got 'em cloze, an' she knows how to weah 'em."

He put the photograph back into a hidden coat pocket and laughed secretively.

The morning customer waited a few minutes and then asked. " How is everything around the place — quiet ?"

" Yes, seh, it 's ve'y quiet 'iss mawnin'. Betteh le' me put in new paih o' laces faw you, misteh. On'y ten cents, seh."

" Well, you go ahead and shine those shoes and we 'll talk about the laces later on."

" Yes, seh, sutny, on'y these heah laces is fah gone."

" Pink, are you criticising my personal appearance ? "

" No, seh, I do n' mean no c'iticizin', on'y if you wan' paih o' laces I know wheah you can get 'em."

" Never mind the laces now. I do n't come here to discuss sordid commercial transactions. Let us lift our conversation into the higher realms. Let's talk about art, or something like that."

" My goodness, misteh, when it comes to me holdin' up my end o' talk 'ith you I 'm no betteh 'n one-legged man at a cake-walk," and he gurgled.

" How are you and Mr. Clifford getting along ? "

" Did n' you heah 'bout it ? Did n' you heah what happen' heah yes'day ? Misteh Cliffo'd done it all, too. He 'uz 'e gen'al an' 'e whole ahmy — yes, seh."

" What was it ? "

"'AT GEMMAN"

" We had wah 'ith Englan' heah yes'day
— O, bad, too. Ouah side win, though.
Gen'al Cliffo'd made wahm fight."

" How did it start? "

" I do n' know. Gen'al Cliffo'd 'uz
settin' oveh theah by 'e table, an' 'fo I
know 'bout it he had ahmy o' fo' million
soljahs an' 'uz mahchin' right oveh to do
Englan'."

" How did he get them across the
ocean? "

" I do n' know, seh. I s'pose he made
'em swim. He had 'em all oveh theah
chasin' 'at English ahmy 'fo' I un'e'stood
what it 'uz all 'bout. Gen'al Cliffo'd 'uz
full o' trouble. He put up betteh fight 'n
Gen'al Grant eveh did. Co'se Misteh
Adams, on 'e thuhd chaih, he'ped some.
Misteh Adams 'uz gen'al of all 'e ships.
I guess it did n' take him mo' 'n ten minutes to sink all of 'em otheh ships. Goodness, mistah, I neveh see such wah in a
bahbeh-shop befo' in all my life."

"What had England been doing?"

"How's 'at? Man, what could ol' Englan' do 'ith Gen'al Cliffo'd an' 'ese fo' million soljahs up an' a' comin'?"

"I know, but why did Mr. Clifford make war on England?"

"It 'uz someping 'bout Venzalum — Venazulum."

"O, Venezuela! Why, that's all settled. Great Britain has agreed to our terms, and the whole difficulty is to be submitted to arbitration."

"Yes, seh, I un'e'stand. Misteh Adams 'uz speakin' to gemman in his chaih 'bout 'iss 'batation 'at Misteh Cliffo'd read 'bout in 'e mawnin' papeh. Misteh Adams tell 'iss gemman 'at 'e reason Englan' lay down is 'at Uni'd States could do 'uh up if it eveh come to case o' scrap. 'En 'iss gemman in Misteh Adams's chaih he says 'at Englan' got mo' ships 'an us an' mo' soljahs, 'an' might do 'iss country if it come to show-down. 'En Misteh Cliffo'd gets

out his fo' million soljahs an' begins.
Goodness, misteh! We jus' had wah faw
'n houah. One minute, you know, Misteh Cliffo'd oveh theah by 'e table he 'd be
killin' 'bout hund'ehd thousan' men and 'en
Misteh Adams at 'e thuhd chaih he put
some of 'ese 'pedoes—"

" Torpedoes."

" Yes, seh, t'pedoes — he 'd put some
o' 'em undeh Englan' ship an' blow 'uh all
to pieces. Misteh Cliffo'd, he say: ' W'y,
do n' talk to me' bout Englan'. We done
huh fo' times an' we can do it agen. I
neveh see a man so wahm faw trouble. All
'iss time Misteh Adams blowin' up ships."

" England had no chance at all ? "

" Misteh, no mo' chance 'an a sheep
'ith a butcheh. You know Gen'al Cliffo'd had eight million men 'fo' he got
th'ough. Yes, seh, I think he got two
hund'ehd thousan' heah in 'iss town. I tell
you, we could n' lose 'e way Gen'al Cliffo'd had it fixed yes'day. 'Fo' he got

43

th'ough he had all 'at Englan' belongin' to
'iss country. You know 'at big town in
Englan'? "

" London? "

" Yes, seh, 'at 's it. How long you
s'pose it took Gen'al Cliffo'd an' his ahmy
to mahch right in an' capchah 'at town? "

" I have n't the slightest idea."

" Two days, seh. Gen'al Cliffo'd an'
his ahmy got oveh theah one day an' 'ey
wuz n' feelin' ve'y well, so 'ey kind o' hang
'round 'e fuhst day loadin' up 'em guns an'
washin' 'e buggies an' 'en nex' mawnin'
'ey go on oveh to London. I think 'ey
got theah 'bout ten o'clock in 'e mawnin'.
'Iss heah gen'al at London he come out
an' size up Gen'al Cliffo'd an' 'ese fo' million white bahbehs, an' tries to put up fight,
but, my goodness, man, 'at gen'al ought to
see his finish 'e minute he go 'genst Gen'al
Cliffo'd. It could n' come out on'y one
way. A little while an' 'em Englishmen
gettin' out of 'e way jus' like cullud boys

"'AT NEW BAHBEH"

goin' out o' Johnson's back dooh afteh razah play — same thing. Gen'al Cliffo'd got on white hoss, misteh, and rode into 'at town 'ith band playin' 'at 'Wash'nin Pos' Mahch.' Yes, seh, 'at secon' day he sutny showed up ve'y strong. He made Gen'al Grant look like lame man."

"In the meanwhile, I suppose Mr. Adams was destroying the English navy — the English ships."

"O, easy, easy, easy! 'Iss same aftehnoon 'at Misteh Cliffo'd — I mean Gen'al Cliffo'd — 'uz ridin' 'e white hoss an' smokin' fifteen-cent cigah, Misteh Adams done up 'e las' English ship — yes, seh, he done up ev'ything. 'Iss gemman in Misteh Adams's chaih he wants to know what Misteh Adams goin' 'o do when 'em English ships come up close to 'at New Yawk City an' staht tossin' wahm cannon balls oveh on 'e houses."

"I suppose Mr. Adams had that all provided for."

"You know it! Yes, seh, 'at wuz an easy one. Misteh Adams got kind o' i'on raft 'at jus' stuck up oveh 'e wateh 'bout foot, an' he took 'iss out to 'at place wheah all 'em otheh ships had to come past, an' 'en ev'y time ship come 'long he'd th'ow ol' dym'nite bum oveh an' blow it up. I guess he blowed up 'bout ten ships in one day. No use tryin', mistch, you can't lose 'at Misteh Adams at no game eveh played. If Englan' eveh fin's out what Misteh Adams got up his sleeve, she won't eveh have no trouble 'ith us, no, seh."

"Well, I am glad to learn that we can whip England."

"W'y, misteh, I tell you we done it already — right heah in 'iss shop yes'day."

"What part did you take in the fratricidal strife?"

"Change it, misteh! Come down!"

"Were you in the fight?"

"No, seh, I set back heah by 'e stove

dodgin' bullets. I neveh see such wah.
'Fo' it 'uz oveh I kind o' felt soh'y faw
'em English people. Did n' have thing
left when Gen'al Cliffo'd got th'ough. Me
an' 'at new bahbeh is 'e on'y ones 'at
wuz n' in 'e wah."

" That's so. You have a new barber,
have n't you ? "

" Yes, seh, I 'm kind o' 'fraid o' him,
too. You see 'at white tie he weahs.
Look out faw 'em, misteh. 'Ey 's eitheh
ve'y good o' ve'y bad 'at weahs 'em white
ties. We had bahbeh heah 'at wo' tie
like 'at one, an' one night 'e got all 'e
razahs in his pockets an' moved. Yes,
seh, he changed his scenery. He 'uz a
quiet boy, too, 'ith one of 'em Zion
Meth'dis' neckties."

" Are you through ? Well, I tell you
what I want, if you have any, and that 's
a pair of new shoe-laces."

" My goodness, misteh ! "

On the Efficacy of Dreams

The next time the morning customer came in he found Pink locked in an earnest debate with Mr. Clifford. The barber was " honing " a razor and debating with careless ease, as one who knew and scorned the full resources of his opponent. Pink had an ominous forefinger in the air and was contending for something or other in relation to civil rights.

" No, seh ! no, seh, I do n' mean 'at, Misteh Cliffo'd," he said. " I do n' mean to 'sinuate 'at a cullud man ought to do anything 'at a white pusson does, but what ahgament I make, Misteh Cliffo'd, is 'at he 's got right to do it undeh ouah law. Did n' Misteh Ab'ham Lincoln settle all 'at business ? I guess he sutny did.

CIVIL RIGHTS

Ab'ham said a few things 'at set 'em guessin'."

" Why, the only mistake we ever made was in settin' you folks free," said Mr. Clifford, with a wink at the barber at the next chair.

Pink laughed aloud, and then said: " O, no, seh, Mistch Cliffo'd, you do n' mean 'at."

" Course I do. You ain't no good when you work for yourself. There 's a man been waitin' in your chair for five minutes while you was talkin' to me."

Pink hurried over to the morning customer with many expressions of apology.

" My goodness, misteh, I did n' see you. I 'm ve'y soh'y, seh. If 'ey 's one thing I prides myself 'bout, seh, it 's bein' right heah, seh, on deck ready faw business at all houahs. 'At 's 'e on'y way to get yo' good customehs an' keep 'em comin' to you, yes, seh. I can't get too many comin' my way, suah as yo' bawn."

" What was all this discussion about?"

" 'At 's all right, misteh ; do n't you feel bad about it an' I won't.   Misteh Cliffo'd got it settled 'ith himse'f 'at he 's ve'y wahm pusson.   No, seh, you could n' make him b'lieve nothin' else.   W'y, misteh, he sets heah ev'y day an' tells 'ese otheh wise boys 'bout what 'at mayah oveh in 'e City Hall ought to do.   If 'at theah mayah 'd on'y come oveh heah ev'y mawnin' an' find out f'om Misteh Cliffo'd how things stood, he sutny could n' make no mistakes.   'Spose Misteh Cliffo'd picks up papeh wheah it tells 'bout a killin'. Well, seh, he reads it oveh, spellin' out 'em long ones — he ain' such a hot readeh — an' when he 's th'ough he tuhns to Misteh Adams an' he say, ' I know who done 'at muhdeh.   It wuz 'at woman 'at find 'e revolveh.'   He knows in a minute. You can't fool 'at boy."

" I think he ought to be chief of police," said the morning customer.

Pink stopped work and shook with suppressed laughter.

" Yo' sutny all right, misteh," said he, " You know, misteh, I can't une'stan' why all 'ese wahm boys 'at knows mo' an' any one else 'at eveh come oveh 'e bridge is all down heah in 'is ol' shop, crawlin' heads faw two bits, when 'ey ought to be up in one of 'em sky-scrapehs — you know, misteh — big desk, an' you push one of 'em bells an' say: ' Boy, take 'bout thousan' dollahs out of 'e safe an' put it in my ovehcoat pocket; I 'm goin' out to meet a few frien's.' 'At 's wheah all 'ese boys 'd be if 'ey wuz half as wahm as 'ey say they ah."

" You do n't seem to have a very high opinion of your tonsorial associates."

" Listen at you toss 'em wuhds !" said Pink, glancing up in rapture. " Otheh foot, misteh. O, well, seh, 'bout white bahbehs — it do n' pay to have no trouble 'ith 'em. Jus' let 'em think 'ey 's 'e real

thing, an' you on'y pooh cullud boy,
tryin' to do 'e best he can, an' yo' all
right. Call 'em misteh so-and-so. 'At's
someping 'ey do n't of'en get an' it jollies
'em. Bu' le' me tell you someping,
misteh. I 'll be eatin' bread 'ith gravy on
it when some of 'ese white bahbehs makin'
mahks in 'e snow."

"By the way, how is your bank account
coming on? You told me, did n't you,
that you were going to begin to save
money after the first of the year?"

Pink leaned over the shoe and
brushed with great energy, but said
nothing. The customer heard sounds
similar to those made by a loose steam-
valve, and upon looking down he saw that
Pink was smothering with laughter,
which he was trying to hold in. This
kind of mirth is contagious. The morning customer began to laugh.

"Misteh, yo' sutny all right," said
Pink, without looking up.

" How much have you saved ? "

" Misteh, all 'ese heah banks can bust an' 'ey wont eveh touch me."

" I thought you were saving up."

" Yes, seh ; 'at s right."

" You've been saving up, but you have n't got anything yet — is that it ? "

" Mistch, if I got it all togetheh I 'd jus' 'bout have pohk chops an' no mo'."

" What have you been doing with your money ? "

" In 'e fus' place, misteh, I do n' take in as much as Misteh Mahshall Field o' Misteh P. D. Ahmoh."

" I see. You've been playing policy again."

" Jus' once in while, seh."

" Have any luck ? "

" Yes, seh ; I come 'ithin one numbeh o' gettin' sisteen dollahs. One ev'nin' at Mis' Willa'd's house we had aigs faw suppeh, fried in fat an' potatoes sliced in. I eat about six o' seven aigs, an' en' all

night dream aigs. I go pas' stoahs an' I
see hund'ehds o' baskets full o' aigs, an' I
think I'm eatin' fried aigs all 'e time ? so
nex' mawnin' I suhch myself an' fin'
twenty cents an' put it on 'e ol' aigs
row."

"Why did n't you play it on the indi-
gestion row ? "

"In'geschun ?" asked Pink, wonder-
ingly.

"Go on with your story. What was
the egg row ? "

"Yes, seh; aig row 'uz fo'-fo'teen-
fawty. Fo' come, misteh, an' ol' fawty,
but fo'teen used me mean."

"How much did you win ? "

"Do n't you un'e'stand 'at game, misteh?
You got to ketch all three. If 'at ol'
fo'teen 'd used me right — say, I'd be
spohtin' ovehcoat 'ith fo' rows o' buttons."

"But fourteen did n't come out, did it?"

"No, seh. 'At dream 'uz all right,
on'y fo'teen would n't come out."

54

" I do n't see what good it did you to have two numbers come, as long as you did n't win."

" It sutny showed 'ey wuz someping in 'at dream."

" All right. I am glad you can see it in that light. Where do you play policy, anyway ? I thought all those places were closed up."

" Misteh, I neveh see time yet when I could n' bet my b'lief, no, seh. You got to weah rubbehs some times to get at 'e man 'ith 'e sheet, but I neveh kep' no money I wanted to lose, not yet, seh."

" Well, that 's a funny thing. I 've lived in this town for ten years, and I never saw a policy-shop yet. I do n't know what one of them would look like."

" Yo' cullah 's wrong, misteh; yo' cullah 's sutny wrong. White pusson can't find 'em games, no matteh how long he hunts, but cullud boy — put blin'fold on him, tuhn him loose in 'at alley, an' he jus' feel his way to some place wheah man's puttin' numbehs on 'e sheet. Cullud boy can smell row o' numbehs faw two blocks. Yes, seh ; 'at 's no fab'cashun, ncethch."

" Fabrication ? That 's a good word."

" 'At 's a ve'y sassy wuhd, misteh. Misteh 'Stein, 'e cigah-man, han' me 'at one yes'day. 'At means yo' lyin', do n' it ? "

" Yes, a fabrication is anomalous to a lie. It is frequently used as a synonym, although if I were to cogitate with exact-itude I would say that it refers rather to a fanciful invention. Of course, you under-stand, Pink, that there are many terms allied in paraphristic connection which are essentially — ah — dissimilar when it comes right down to it. Have you got change for a quarter ? Thanks. Well, I must meander toward my destination. That 's a good shine you gave me. I hope you will not become egotistical by reason

"MISTEH 'STEIN"

of my eulogiums. By George! It's nearly nine o'clock."

The morning customer hurried toward the door, leaving Pink open-mouthed and staring into vacancy. He was in a waking dream, and the broom swung in his limp hand. His lips moved, but no sound came forth.

On the Powers of the Chief Executive

From the day on which the morning customer defined the word " fabrication " he became the court of last resort. On the occasion of his first succeeding visit he was called on to settle a dispute.

" Misteh, I want you to tell me someping, 'cuz I know you can tell it to me right," began Pink.

" I do n't know that I can. You must n't ask me anything hard."

" 'At 's all right, seh. If I had yo' ej'cation I would n' be scaihed o' no question in 'e book. If I on'y had as many fac's in my head as you got I 'd win mo'n one bet f'om some of 'em wise Af'o-Ameh'cans out theah on Deahbohn Street."

"You 've got Afro-Americans out there, have you?"

"Yes, seh; I neveh know I 'uz one of 'em till 'bout two weeks ago. Ain't safe to call cullud man coon no mo' any mo' 'an it is to say ' niggeh.' My goodness, misteh! Do n' like to be called dahkies neetheh. It use to be Eth'op'ans, but now it 's Af'o-Ameh'cans. 'At 's a ve'y wahm name. Since 'ey begin to use 'at name I would n' change my cullah faw no money.'

"What is the dispute you were asking about?"

"Yes, seh. I tell you. It 'uz a 'spute I had 'tween me an' Willis Tuckeh at Miss Willa'd's house last ev'nin'. Willis begin by askin' me who I 'd ratheh be, Misteh Presiden' McKinley o' Misteh Potteh Palmeh. I say I ratheh be Misteh McKinley, faw even if I did n' have as much money I could give p'sitions to all my frien's an' get good livin' faw nothin'. Willis want to know how I figgah

it, an' I say 'at 'e Presiden of 'iss heah
land can say to any man he likes, ' Heah,
you go to Eu'ope faw me an' spend all 'e
money you need an' have good time.'
'Notheh thing, too, I say, Misteh McKinley he get anything he wants f'om 'e
gov'ment. If he want new fuhnichah in
'e house wheah he lives he jus' send out an'
get it an' have 'e bill sent to Cong'ess. It
don' cost him a cent. He sutny have a
snap, I say. Now, misteh, I want to
know am I right what I say 'bout 'e Presiden'."

" Well, what did Willis say ? "

" Yes, seh, Willis claim to me Misteh
McKinley could n' buy nothin' 'ceptin'
Cong'ess say it 'uz all right. I tell him,
' Man, yo' foolish; 'at Presiden' comes
puht neah bein' 'e whole thing 'bout 'iss
gov'ment.' You le' me be Presiden' faw
twenty minutes some time an' I would n'
neveh shine no mo' shoes f' no man."

" That's right. I suppose you 'd order

"WILLIS TUCKEH"

everything in sight, and have it charged up to Congress."

"Hush, man! I would n' do thing! 'At's what I tell Willis. I say Mistch Presiden' McKinley can buy anything he wants an' Cong'ess got to pay faw it. Willis say Presiden' got to ask Cong'ess 'bout it befo'-hand an' 'en if 'ey say it's all right, he goes 'head an buys it."

"I do n't think Willis knows very much about the functions of the Executive."

"Fum-shun? Say, misteh, if I could say 'at jus' 'e way you done it I would n' let Willis Tuckeh o' no otheh man sew me up in no ahgament, no, seh. What's 'at you mean by 'at 'bout fum-shun?"

"I mean that your friend Willis is mistaken. That would be a fine state of affairs, would n't it—the President of the United States going around to Congress to get a little money every time he wants to buy some groceries?"

" Misteh, you know I use 'most 'em
ve'y wuhds to Willis Tuckeh? I claim,
seh, 'at no man has mo' to say 'bout 'e
gov'ment 'an Misteh Presiden' McKinley.
Am I true in 'at ? "

" Certainly you are. You tell your
friend to go and read the constitution of
the United States."

" Who — Willis Tuckeh? No, seh;
he ain' no friend o' mine. I 'm jus' ready
heah an' now to buy ticket to his fune'al.
Yes, seh—he done me duht."

" You appear to cherish an animosity
toward Mr. Tucker."

" I got 'mosity faw any man 'at hol's
out on you. Yes, seh, what 'at speckled
houn' done to me I ain' goin' 'o fawget
ve'y soon."

" What 's your grievance? "

" I do n' say I grieve 'bout it. When
he say to me, ' No, seh, Pink, 1 did n' get
it on,' I jus' say, ' O!' — like 'at — an'
p'ten' like to believe him, but I know con

when I get it. 'Ey can make me take it, misteh, but no man can't make me like it — no, sch!''

" What was it he was supposed to 'get on ' ? "

" I tell you, seh. 'Bout fo' weeks ago, I dream nothin' but flowehs. I seem walkin' in fields 'ith nothin' but jus' flowehs as fah as I could see. I 'd see sunflowehs and mawnin'-glo'ies an' pinks an' ev'y kind o' flowehs — mo'n I eveh seen befo' in all my life. Well, seh, nex' mawnin' I kep' thinkin' 'bout 'em flowehs, an' I say, ' 'At sutny means someping.' Afteh breakfas' I stops in at Clem Lesteh's bahbeh-shop on State Street an' see in his book 'at if you dream wil' flowehs, 'e row is three — seven — twenty-eight, an' if it 's flowehs done up in bo'quets, you want to play nine — thuhty — fift'-two. Well, seh, I seen all kind o' flowehs, so I jus' say I play wil' flowahs an' bo'quets, both.''

" What is this play — policy again? "

" Yes, seh, two rows, jus' as I say, one faw wil' flowehs an' one faw bo'quets. I 'uz jus' goin' out of 'e shop an' I meet Willis Tuckeh. I say, ' Willis, I got to huh'y down to 'e shop an' J want you to take quahteh an' split it on two sets o' numbehs I got heah. I had 'em wrote down, misteh, an' I give 'em to him. I play nick in Frankfo't book f' three — seven — twenty-eight and straddle ten 'tween Frankfo't an' Kentucky on same row and let 'e otheh dime go on straddle f' nine — thuhty — fift'-two. Willis p'omised me he'd see 'at 'e money got on faw afteh-noon drawin'.''

" And then he did n't do it, eh? "

" Yes, seh, he done it, an' 'at's what makes me soah. W'y, misteh, when I get th'ough my wuhk 'at day an' go to Misteh Lesteh's shop and see ol' nine an' ol' thuhty an' ol' fift'-two all in 'e row on 'e sheet, I could jus' see myse'f countin' money. My goodness, misteh, I ask faw Willis,

THE MORNING CUSTOMER

an' no one seen him. I go oveh to his
house. 'No,' Mis' Tuckeh say, 'I ain't
seen Willis since mawnin'. So I stahts
'long 'e line. I want to save some of 'at
eight. Last I fin' Willis in 'Lias Clahk's
saloon rubbin' 'genst 'e bah an' two crap-
playehs along. Jus' soon 's I see 'at
boy, misteh, I knowed it wuz n' no watch
made 'em eyes 'at cullah. Cullud man
can't get red in 'e face, but his eyes get
bad, an' ol' Willis he had Tom gin eyes
when I find him. I say, 'Willis, will
you give 'em to me in papeh o' silveh?'
He act su'prise like an' say, 'What you
talkin' 'bout?' I say, ''At secon' row win
in 'e Frankfo't book.' Well, seh, when
I said 'bout winnin', he made 'e wahmes'
bluff I eveh see. O, he's good, Willis
is. He says, 'By Gawge, Pink, I clean
fawgot to get 'em numbehs,' an' 'en he
han' me back 'at nasty ol' quahteh. I
made no holleh, misteh. I neveh let on,
but did n' I know 'at man had my right-

ful money right in his cloze? I went
'roun' to 'e policy-shop to look at 'e bet-
sheet, but ol' Willis 'uz too keen faw me.
He'd gone an' bet it somewheahs else.
Yes, seh, he done me up. My goodness,
misteh, I get so mad ev'y time I re'lize
'bout lettin' him do me. He done me
right, suah. Un'e'stand, if numbehs did n'
come, ol' Willis say to me, ' Heah's 'e
tickets, Pink,' an' 'en he hand you some
dead numbehs. If 'e row *did* come, he
cash in an' keep all 'e velvet an' gi' me
back my coin. Misteh, I jus' figgah I
did n' have no show faw my life 'ith 'at
man."

" I suppose not. I'm surprised, however, that any of your Afro-American ac-
quaintances would be guilty of such du-
plicity."

" 'Plicity, misteh? I wan' tell you,
Willis Tuckeh's wuhse 'an 'at. He's
chicken-lifteh. When he goes 'long an

alley, chickens come out an' roost on him.
I know all 'bout his cha'cteh now. He
can't neveh place no mo' money faw me.
No, seh!"

On the Origin of Species

After a brief experience as oracle to Pink, the morning customer decided to be infallible. He learned that Pink came to him with full trust, and he believed it the better plan to answer all questions. So he found it his task to settle the problems relating to life and the after-life. Such a task would have been difficult but for the fact that Pink hung upon his words in simple faith and was not disposed to cross-question. One morning the subject matter was evolution.

" Misteh, I 'm goin 'o ask you someping 'at me an' Misteh Cliffo'd 'uz 'sputin' 'bout 'iss mawnin'," said Pink, pouring some of the soft dressing into the clay-colored bowl of his hand. " Misteh Cliffo'd says 'at 'iss heah Bob Inge'soll

claim 'at all cullud people use to be suah-
'nough monks, same as 'ey got out heah
at Lincum Pahk."

" The theory of evolution is that all
men came from the lower orders of
animal life," said the morning customer.
" If Mr. Clifford says that the colored
people in particular are descendants of
the simian, he is laboring under a misap-
prehension."

" I tol' Misteh Cliffo'd he 'uz givin'
me mis'plehension, 'cuz you know, I may
be easy, but 'ey can't shoot nothin' like
'at into me, no, seh."

" Does Mr. Clifford believe in evolution ? "

" Mistah, what is 'at emvalution ? "

" I believe it is defined as a change,
by continuous differentiation and integra-
tion, from a simple homogeneity to a com-
plex heterogeneity, or something like
that."

" All right, misteh, heah 's wheah I get

off. 'Iss is my cohneh. Goodness, man!
You ah sutny holdin' back mo' good talk
an' any pusson I eveh see. 'Ferenchia-
shum of 'genity — I guess 'at 's pooh talk,
ain't it? I 'm glad you handed 'at to me.
I been kind o' wantin' to get 'at cleahed
up in my mind. I know it now, misteh.
Need n' say it agen."

The morning customer lifted the newspaper to conceal his grin of self-satisfac-
tion, and Pink labored at the shoe, occa-
sionally shaking his head and whispering
to himself.

Finally he looked up and said, " I tol'
Misteh Cliffo'd I could n't un'e'stand 'at,
'cuz I know 'at ol' Adam was 'e fus' man
of all. Ain't 'at so ? "

" That 's right. We all descended
from Adam."

" Yes, seh, an' Misteh Cliffo'd ask me
how it is 'at we got white people an' cullud people. He kind o' had me guessin'.
How 'bout 'at, misteh ? "

" Why, that 's easy enough. We were all white once, but some of the people went down into Africa just after the flood, and it was so hot down there that they became tanned."

"You call 'at tan?" asked Pink, thoughtfully looking at his knuckles, which resembled a row of chocolate creams. " No, seh, misteh, 'at ain't no tan. You sutny got to skin me to change my cullah. No, seh. Huh-uh! S'pose I go in Audito'um hotel to get dinneh 'an 'e whole thing 'ith one of 'em Gawgy minstrel suits come up an' say, ' Niggeh, you get out 'o heah befo' we take you out piece at a time!' I say, ' S'cuse me, seh, I 'm no niggeh: I 'm white man 'at got sunbuhned!' Co'se 'at 'd be all right! He 'd un'e'stand 'at! Any man look at me know 'ey 's nothin' 'e matteh 'cept I 'm kind o' flushed f'om bein' outdoohs."

" Well, I do n't deny that the color is fixed now, but you must remember that it required many generations for the African to assume his present color."

" Yes, seh, it's goin' 'o be two o' three yeahs 'fo' I change back to be blonde too," said Pink, and he gave an explosive bark of laughter.

" What 's the matter with you, over there ? " asked the new barber, with the white tie, who was sea-foaming a red-headed man and getting some good color-effects.

" Neveh you mind," returned Pink, " I 'm findin' out things. Look heah, misteh, how is it some cullud people 's so dahk an' othehs jus' yellow ? I s'pose some of 'em set in 'e shade mo' 'an othehs."

" I do n't know, I 'm sure," said the morning customer, trying to restrain a smile.

" I guess 'at what you say 'bout changin' cullah ain't so fah off, neetheh. I use' to know cullud boy in Tuhkish bath place

A "CREOLE"

'at got job on 'e stage doin' buck-dancin',
an' some of 'at pasamala wahm stuff. He
could jus' melt 'e nails out of 'e flooh,
Albe't could. Ev'ybody thought Albe't
'uz a cullud boy till 'e got 'iss job 'ith
'e show. W'y, he wuz n' no coon at all,
no, seh."

" What was he ? "

" Yes, seh; he wuz a creole, 'at 's
what Albe't wuz. Co'se you look at
Albe't an' you might think 'at he had
some niggeh blood in him, but he ain't.
No, seh, he 's a creole. I know it, 'cuz
I see it on 'e show-bills. Good many
people 'at used to be cullud is tuhnin'
out to be creoles, oct'oons, Eth'op'ans,
Af'o-Ameh'cans, an'—

" Any Cubans ? "

" Yes, seh, some — smoked Cubans.
Goodness, misteh, you can't hahdly find
no mo' coons on 'e South Side. I think I
betteh be creole myse'f, same as Albe't."

" How are you on dancing, Pink ? "

" Wahm — wahm, an' no mistake.
You neveh see me pick 'em up an' set 'em
down agen, did you ? I fool you, misteh;
I ain't so bad. No, seh ! But I sutny
got to hang my head when ol' Albe't
begin movin' 'round in 'e sand. Albe't
got me faded, suah. Albe't went up to
rent-rag 'ith me one night, an' win ev'y
woman in 'e house. I guess 'ey wuz
mo' 'an a dozen razahs shahpened faw ol'
Albe't 'at night."

" What in the world is a rent-rag ? "

" You do n' know what a rent-rag is,
misteh ? I guess you ain't been out 'round
Deahbohn Street ve'y much. You see,
misteh, 'ey's quite a numbah o' cullud
fam'lies 'at 's hahd up 'iss time o' yeah,
an' 'ey can't ve'y well come up 'ith 'e
rent. So 'ey have pahties, an' chahge
ev'y one someping to come in — ten cents
sometimes, o' as much as two bits. 'At 's
'e way some of 'em got to do to stand off
'e lan'lohd. Ev'ybody comes in and has

good time, an' 'e fam'ly 's two or three
dollahs to 'e good. Yes, seh, we had
some ve'y wahm sessions at 'em rent-rags.
'Ey 's sutny good. Take it 'bout two
'clock in 'e mawnin' 'ith all of 'em po'tehs
and waitehs kind o' crackin' 'ith Tom gin,
I tell you it ain't safe to staht nothin'.
'At 's what I say: ' Be good, but do n'
staht nothin' 'cuz anything stahted it 's
goin' 'o finish at 'e hospital, suah 's yo'
bawn.' 'Long 'bout two you got to be
caihful whose lady you lay yo' hand on.
'Cuz I know. I see Grant Jenkins pull
his 'ol bahbeh's friend one night, and begin
makin' signs at ol' Gawge Lippincott's
brotheh, 'at 'uz visitin' heah f'om In'ana-
polis, an', misteh, you jus' ought to see
Pink come down 'em staihs. O, I guess
I wuz slow, wuz n' I? I did n' wait to
walk down. No, seh; I wuz too busy.
I jus' fell, 'at 's all I done. If 'ey 's eveh
goin' 'o be any cahvin', misteh, I jus' soon
go home an' 'en read 'bout it in 'e papeh

nex' mawnin'. Yes, seh; I do n' mind waitin' to find out what 'e finish is."

" You must be associated with a desperate crowd."

" No, seh; 'em boys ain't tough on'y faw a few 'at gets mixed in. I been to some of 'em pahties out theah 'at uz 'e real thing, misteh. Yes, seh; most ev'y one have on 'em dress suits. 'At 's wheah they lose me, misteh. Most all of 'em cullud waitehs got to have 'em suits befo' they can wuhk. Ol' Pink shows up 'ith his blue cloze an' he ain't one-two-three. Guess I 'll have to be waiteh if I 'm goin' 'o be strong out theah. I ain' sayin' a wuhd, but I 'm jus' layin' faw a suit of 'em cloze 'at some white gemman 's got th'ough usin'. You eveh le' me get a suit of 'em real boys, misteh, an 'ey 's nothin' on 'e South Side goin' 'o pass me — no, seh. I 'll put some of 'em coffee-cullud waitehs in a trance, 'cuz 'em suits 'ey flash is bad—got grease-spots all down 'e front."

"SUAH–'NOUGH SPOHT"

"How would you like to have a suit with silk facing on the lapels?" asked the morning customer.

"Hush, man, hush! Do n' get me to dreamin'."

"I've got a dress-suit you can have if you want it."

"Look out, man! Be caihful! Do n' say it 'less you mean it, 'cuz 'at 's jus' what I 'm needin'."

"I mean it. I had to buy a new suit a few weeks ago. The old one 's up there at the room, and you can have it any time you come for it."

"Misteh, I be theah 'iss aftehnoon ahead o' you, I p'omise you that."

"All right. I do n't know whether it will fit you or not. I think you 're a little larger than I am."

"It 's got to fit me, misteh. I need it, an' it 's got to fit me. I won' do a thing 'ith 'at ol' suit nex' Satuhday night, I guess."

" What is it—a rent-rag?"

" No, seh; 'e Sons an' Daughtehs o' Estheh goin' 'o have dance at Temp'ance Hall. I guess I won' be theah at all."

" O, I see. You are going to execute a social *coup de main*."

" I 'll be wuhse 'n 'at, misteh. I 'll make 'em cheap waiteh's put on theah ovehcoats an' go home."

The morning customer wrote his home address on a card.

That evening he found Pink waiting at the front gate. The suit of evening clothes, with the real silk facing on the coat, was wrapped up in a newspaper and handed out to the boy, who did fancy walking steps as he went away, keeping time to his own music.

On the Pride Which Goes Before
a Fall

There was a strange face in the corner. Pink was missing.

The morning customer hesitated for a moment, and then he climbed up on the throne and sat in the saggy arm-chair.

" Shine ? " asked the new boy.

" No, I want to be manicured," replied the morning customer.

The colored youth stood still and looked at the man in the chair. He seemed to be in doubt.

" Do n' you want no shine ? " he asked.

" Of course I want a shine."

Pink's successor settled down on the stool as if in a general collapse, and began to sponge mud from the shoe on the foot-rest.

He was tall and loose-jointed. His
color was that of coffee not yet roasted.
The forelock of his kinky hair stood up
like a steeple. Instead of a shirt he
wore a cotton sweater, which had been
white at one time. His brown coat was
short for him, and the black braid had been
worn away in places. The trousers were
a shiny black.

He went at his work slowly and solemnly. The morning customer leaned
his elbows on the arms of the chair and
studied him. Then he asked: "Where
is the boy who was here last week?"

"I dunno."

"Is he sick?"

"I dunno."

"How did you happen to get this job?"

"Well, seh, he did n' show up yes'day
mawnin'. I guess he's fiahed."

"What's your name?"

"Edwahd Petehs."

"All right, Eddie. Will you just hurry

THE SUCCESSOR

a bit ? Your technique is good, but your tempo is bad."

The new boy looked up sleepily and made no response. He toiled patiently, but the shine which he imparted was nothing more than a dull, metallic burnish.

The morning customer passed upon him and decided that he was tired, wobbly, and uninteresting.

And where was Pink ?

Mr. Clifford was not at the shop, so the morning customer applied to Mr. Adams for information. Mr. Adams, who was chewing gum and looking at a colored weekly, did not trouble himself to look up when the question was addressed to him. He smiled in fixed admiration at a noisy cartoon and said, " The old man let him go."

The morning customer went back to his office feeling that a part of his morning had been wasted.

It was about two o'clock in the afternoon

when the office-boy came to the door and said, " Colored feller wants to see you."

" A colored fellow? Who is he? What does he want to see me about?"

"I do n't know. He 's got one hand wrapped up."

" Well, I can't imagine — tell him to come in."

With hesitating steps William Pinckney Marsh came to the doorway. His overcoat collar was turned up, and one of his hands was bound up in a rude bandage, which was fastened with a large safety-pin. He had a sorrowful gaze. His eyeballs were threaded and bloodshot.

The morning customer repressed an unfeeling inclination to laugh. He put himself on his dignity and asked: " O, it 's you, is it, Pink?"

" Yes, seh; jus' some pieces o' me, 'at 's all."

" Sit down."

Pink eased himself down into a chair,

shook his head as if in bitterness of spirit, and gave a gusty sigh.

"What's this I hear about you losing your job?" asked the morning customer.

"I'm a good thing, misteh," said Pink, soothing the bandaged hand.

"You don't seem to be particularly joyous about it. Have you had any trouble?"

"Misteh, I ain' had nothin' else. No use talkin', I stahted out to do too much in one night. I stahted bold, misteh, but I sutny got lost at 'e finish."

"Well, my time is valuable, Pink. If you have any tale of woe, why, go ahead with it."

"Misteh, it 'uz 'at dress-suit you give me. I wanted to be too good, too good."

"Did you go to the ball?"

"'At's wheah I stahted faw, misteh. I stahted all right. I wuz goin' to take 'at Miss Lo'ena Jackson to 'e pahty of 'at Sons an' Daughtehs o' Estheh. I got on 'em cloze you give me, an' I look myse'f oveh an' say: 'O, I guess I'm pooh.' Yes, seh, I wuz too wahm. Stahted out good, on'y I wanted to make flash befo' some of 'em boys 'at hangs out at Mahtin's — yes, seh."

" Martin's being, I presume, a saloon kept by a gentleman of your own color?"

"Yes, seh," said Pink, weakly. "I goes in Mahtin's, an' I see Clay Walkeh an' some mo' boys rollin' 'e bones. I go up to Clay, an' I say: 'What's yo' point?' He say: 'Nine.' I say, 'Two bits you seven,' an' he done it. Misteh, I pick up my two frien's an' breathe on 'em an—"

"Look here, Pink," said the morning customer, glancing at the clock on top of the desk, " I have n't time to follow you through the intricacies of a crap game. What happened?"

" Misteh, 'em dice did n' have nothin' but sevens faw me. I win eight dollahs fast as I could pick money up. I could n'

quit aftch I got 'at much, not 'ithout takin'
chances. Yes, seh, I had on 'em cloze,
an' ev'ything comin' my way, an' I could n'
get 'em drinks fast enough. Gin an' honey,
'at 's what I wuz throwin' in."

" Then you became intoxicated ? "

" Misteh, I fawgot Miss Lo'ena Jackson
an' 'at pahty. 'Em cloze made me too
good. I wuz gamblin' 'ith race-hoss boys
an' suah-'nough spohts, an' I would n' let
no man pass me."

" How did you hurt your hand ? "

" Yes, seh, 'at 's wheah gemman tried to
do me 'ith a pokeh."

" That 's pleasant. And how did you
come to lose your job ? "

" Misteh, I woke up 'bout ten 'clock
nex' mawnin' on a table in 'at back room
at Mahtin's."

" All your money gone, I suppose."

" Do n't ask, man; do n't ask."

" So you did n't show up for work ? "

" Yes, seh, 'at 's jus' what I done an'

'ey had 'notheh boy on 'e chaih. Misteh Cliffo'd sen' me out of 'e shop, 'cuz he say I wuz n' sobeh yet."

" I expect he was right. What are you going to do now? Have you got another job?"

" No, seh; I 'm sutny on 'e edge of 'at cahpet, misteh."

" You remember what I told you about saving your money? If you had a little money in the bank now, you 'd be all right."

" Yes, seh, if I had some money in 'e bank, I would n' caih so much to get wuhk right away."

" I expect not. There 's no need of working as long as you have a cent any-where on earth. Well, what are you go-ing to do?"

" Misteh, I want to write letteh to Misteh Cliffo'd, an' say 'at if he'll put me back on 'e chaih, I 'll sutny conduc' myse'f as gemman should in a bahbeh-shop."

" Yes, — and what else do you want to tell him ? "

" Yes, seh, I say to tell Misteh Cliffo'd 'at I 'm a man among men, an' neveh inten' to do no pusson no hahm, and if he hiahs me back in 'at shop I 'll sutny g'antee to conduc' myse'f sa'sfacto'y."

" All right."

The morning customer touched a pushbutton, and a young woman came in from the outer room with a book in her hand.

" Take this," said he, and after the young woman had seated herself he dictated as follows :

MR. CLIFFORD — Dear Sir: "To err is human; to forgive, divine." Your petitioner beseeches you from a contrite heart to forgive and forget his recent wandering from the straight and narrow path.   He admits that, as a result of circumstances which cannot be set forth in this connection, he partook too freely of alcoholic stimulants, and thereby rendered himself incapable of appearing at your establishment at the customary hour to assume the duties allotted to him. Mr. Clifford, remember what the poet says: "Judge not, but rather in your heart let gentle pity dwell."

I am a man among men, and if you should deem it advisable to reinstate me in the responsible position which I held in your tonsorial apartments, I can assure you that I will so conduct myself as to promote your business interests and bring the glad flush of pleasure to the cheek of your most fastidious patron. Do not condemn a young man for all time because of one offense. Never before, during my entire occupancy of the position at your establishment, did I forget the ancient glory of my race or my own standing as an Afro-American, and allow myself to fall into the clutches of the rum fiend. Now that I have come to a new realization of the scriptural line, "At the last it biteth like a serpent and stingeth like an adder," I am fully determined to abstain from all spirituous, vinous or malt intoxicating liquors, and especially gin and honey.

I am credibly informed that the gentleman who has succeeded me, and who is now mak-

"TOO GOOD! TOO GOOD!"

ing a pitiable attempt to win the favor of the
public, is not an artist of any standing, and
that his work has been the subject of severe
criticism. Therefore, I humbly request that
the past be forgotten, and that we soon re-
sume those relations which were productive
of pleasure to me and, I am quite sure, of some
pecuniary profit to you. I have the extreme
honor to subscribe myself, very truly and affec-
tionately,

" Now, when she gets that written out,
you can sign it," said the morning customer.

Pink had been listening to the dictation
with such consuming interest that his
eyes were set and staring, and his lower
lip hung down and out like a drooping red
petal. When the morning customer
spoke to him he blinked and shook his
head slowly as if he were coming out of
heavy slumber.

" If 'at letteh do n' put me back, it jus'
means I can't be put, 'at 's all," said he.

On the Relative Merits of Great Contemporaries

Three days after the dictation of the letter, the morning customer received a postal-card which read as follows:

Yore letter got me my job back. Old cusstomers always welcom. Yours truely,

WILLIAM PINCKNEY MARSH.

He laughed, and sent the card out to his stenographer.

Next morning he did not go to Mr. Clifford's shop. He knew that if he seemed over-willing to promote an intimacy, Pink would no longer hold him in awe.

On the second morning he went to the shop. Pink arose from the corner smiling expectantly, but the morning customer responded with a conservative nod, and climbed into the chair without speaking. He knew that if he encouraged familiarity at this crisis, he might lose his place as an oracle, and certainly he would cease to be a height.

Pink was somewhat abashed by the coolness of his patron. He went to work quietly, and after a while he said: " Well, seh, I 'm back heah."

" So I see. I trust it is with the determination to make amends for the past."

" You know me, misteh. Jus' watch me lay low."

" You and Mr. Clifford are once more on friendly terms? "

" My goodness, misteh, jus' like brothehs. Yes, seh, Misteh Cliffo'd say I can have 'iss job jus' long as I keep sobeh. Drink it, misteh? Huh-uh! ' Come on, Pink, an' have someping.' ' No, seh, 'at stuff used me wrong—don' wan' no mo' of 'at.' "

" No more gin and honey, eh? "

" Hush, misteh! 'At 's bad—bad! Gin an' honey 's bad, misteh. It is sutny smooth bev'age, but it hahms you jus' like 'at five-cent whisky. Ain' got no claws while it 's goin' down, misteh, but you get it to wuhkin', an' you want to get right out an' fight yo' own fam'ly. Do n' do thing to you, no, seh."

" When did you get back here? "

" Day befo' yes'day mawnin', misteh. 'At letteh you got up faw me fix it 'ith Misteh Cliffo'd. My goodness, 'at 'uz a wahm boy, suah ! Some of 'em wuhds you tossed into Misteh Cliffo'd neveh come out o' no small book, no, seh. 'Em 'uz 'e real tomolleys. Some of 'em too good f' Misteh Cliffo'd, an' he kind o' guesses 'at he 's 'e real thing, too."

Just then there was an outbreak at the other end of the room. The barber with the white tie was waving paper money and telling Mr. Adams that he must either " put up or shut up." Mr. Adams ap-

"WATCH ME LAY LOW"

peared to be in a scornful mood. He walked toward his own chair and made a side remark, to the effect that it was a "bluff." Thereupon the barber with the white tie laughed defiantly and put the money back into his pocket.

"What's the matter with those gentlemen?" asked the morning customer.

"Do n't you know what 'at is? 'Em wise boys is settlin' 'at fight next week. Yes, seh, 'ey been bettin' jus' like 'at all day yes'day an' to-day, an' I ain't seen no money go up yet. 'Em boys is full o' spohtin' blood."

"Well, what do you think of the fight yourself?"

"Misteh, it's bet'een two of 'em cheap white fightehs, an' it do n' make no dif-f'ence who wins. S'pose Misteh Cliffo'd knock out Misteh Adams—'at do n' show nothin'. It's jus' like goin' into 'at side-show an' thinkin' you see 'e real suhcus."

"What do you mean by that?"

" You know well 'nough what I mean, misteh — man like you 'at reads all 'bout 'ese boys in 'e papehs. I mean 'ey 's one ol' boy 'at can jus' fold 'em up an' lay 'em away as fast as you hand 'em to him, yes, seh."

" Do you mean Sullivan ?"

" Listen to you talk ! No, seh ! I do n' mean no John L. I mean 'e wahmest one at eveh wuz—Peteh Jackson."

" O, Peter Jackson? He was a good man."

"Make it betteh 'n good, misteh ; make it strongeh. He 'uz 'at ol' teacheh, Peteh wuz, an' all 'em otheh boys had to go to school to 'im. Any time ol' Peteh get licked, all 'em cullud boys 'long Ahmoh Av'nue an' Deahbohn Street sutny goin' 'o stahve. Anybody goin' 'o do Peteh betteh get razah an' a gun."

" I was under the impression that he and Corbett fought a draw once."

" Look heah, misteh ! Do n't you

know 'bout 'at draw? Peteh had his leg
broke an' could n' get at Misteh Cawbett.
Peteh eveh ketch up 'ith 'at pompado' boy
— all off, suah! Peteh eveh push Misteh
Cawbett 'ith one of 'em big black hams —
Misteh Cawbett would n' be lookin' f'
no fight 'ith Mr. Fitz now, no, seh. He'd
jus' 'bout be gettin' out of 'at hospital."

" Oh, I think you're prejudiced in favor
of Peter on account of his color. He's
out of it now."

" Well, seh, if he *is* out of it 'at's
mighty good thing faw some of 'ese boy
fightehs. 'Cuz if Peteh eveh comes back
'iss way, somebody has sutny got to be eat,
yes, seh!"

" Did you ever see Peter?"

" Hush, man! Did I? I took a drink
'ith Misteh Peteh Jackson one day down
at Johnson's. You see Peteh walk into
'at place an' ev'y Pullman po'tch an'
lunch-room boy jus' drop down on his
knees and shake like 'at. Ol' Will Ah-

buckle — say, misteh! Ol' Will Ahbuckle he spah 'ith cullud fellow f'om
Milwaukee oveh heah on 'e lake front
one night, an' he got it all fixed 'ith himse'f
'at he wuz suah-nough p'ize fighteh. One
day he wuz stan'in at 'e bah in Johnson's
tellin' a lot of 'em cheap yellow boys how
to get in 'ith 'at knock-out. My goodness, misteh, he wuz makin' all 'em sassy
swings an' uppeh-cuts — oh, he wuz good!
All o' sudden 'em boys' eyes kind o' bug
out an' some one say : ' Look out, Will,
'at 's him now.' ' Who is it?' ol' Will
hollehs, swingin' round — bad, you know.
Somebody tol' him it wuz Peteh Jackson.
My goodness, misteh, you jus' ought to
seen — tuhned kind o' white, suah. He
neveh said 'notheh wuhd all 'e time Misteh
Peteh Jackson 'uz theah. He jus' kep'
still an' give him 'at eye. Oscah Jones
says Will neveh did get to be as black
agen as he wuz 'at day Peteh walked
in."

" So you 're not taking much interest in this coming fight ? "

" Jus' side-show, misteh, 'at 's all. Can't have no suah-'nough p'ize fight 'ithout ol' Peteh bein' theah. Co'se Gawge Dixon's puhty wahm boy, an' 'at Misteh Joe Woolcott ain't so cold, but 'ey 's on'y one hot baby, misteh, an' 'at 's Misteh Peteh Jackson f'om Aust'alia."

" You seem to think that the Afro-Americans are invincible."

" How 's 'at, misteh ? "

" I say, you seem to think that a colored man can 't be defeated."

" On'y way to lick cullud man, misteh, is to ketch him on 'e shin."

" On the shin ? Does that hurt ? "

" Huht, man? My goodness ! You see Polk Street coppeh takin' in one of 'em bad boys f'om 'e levee — he do n't hit him on no head. He jus' rap him one 'cross 'e shin an' 'at cullud boy lay down an' yell jus' like he been shot. Cullud boy

sutny can't stan' nothin' on his shin. I
see cullud boy f'om Palmeh House put
on 'e gloves one night 'ith white fellow
down heah at Batte'y D, misteh. 'At
white man he pound 'at cullud boy on 'e
head till his knuckles all broke, an' 'e
cullud boy kep' on comin' back an' askin'
faw mo'. 'En when 'at ref'ee wuz n'
lookin', 'at white man spiked 'e cullud boy
on 'e shin. Misteh, he could n' get 'em
gloves off soon 'nough. Yes, seh,
misteh, you eveh have any trouble 'ith a
cullud boy, you get up as neah to him as
you can an' say, ' 'At 's all right, seh, we
do n' want no ahgament,' an' 'en you get
in hot one on his shin befo' he has time to
reach f' anything. You got him licked,
suah."

"Well, that 's very interesting, but I
do n't expect to have any altercations with
colored men."

"I do n' know, seh. You can't tell,
misteh. One of 'em fresh ones come in

State street cah an' set down in yo' lap an'
you got to notice him. You jus' got to
do it."

The morning customer made no response. In a few moments Pink looked
up and said :

" Misteh, ah yo' too busy mos' all time
to get me up 'notheh letteh?"

" Who is it this time?"

" Yes, seh; 'at lady I tol' you 'bout one
day heah."

" I remember. What was her name?"

" Miss Lo'ena Jackson."

" No relation to Peter, eh?"

" No, seh, but she 's jus' as wahm."

" This is the girl who expected you to
buy a bicycle for her."

" 'At 's 'e one, misteh. She 's been
ridin' 'at wheel ev'y night 'iss winteh
while she wuz 'sleep. I kind o' queeah
myse'f 'ith Lo'ena 'at night I wuz goin' 'o
take huh to 'at pahty of 'em Sons an'
Daughtehs 'o Estheh. No use talkin';

99

I need one of 'em hot lettehs to squaih it. I need it bad. If you jus' want to get up someping 'at 'll fix 'at lady, w'y, you know me, seh. I 'm a pusson 'at 'peciates any good deed done to me, an' I show any consid'ation possible."

" I 'll think it over," said the morning customer, dryly. " I think it 's best to keep you on probation for a while."

" Well, seh, you know me, seh," said Pink, as the morning customer arose. " I gen'ally try to be man among men, and you 'll find 'at my p'obation is sutny all right. Good mawnin', seh."

"WILL AHBUCKLE"

On Man's Love of Power and Dominion

Now, although the morning customer did not aspire to become private secretary to Pink, combining the duties of that office with his continuous task as oracle, he felt it to be his bounden duty to compose a letter to Miss Lorena Jackson. He did not attempt to excuse Pink's conduct on the night of the reception given by the Sons and Daughters of Esther, and he admitted to himself that Pink had practiced a confidence game on Miss Jackson by his implied promise to give her a bicycle. Pink was not worthy, that seemed certain, and yet the morning customer forgave him, in that easy charity which enables us to forgive so many sins that are not directly against us. He prepared a letter, and when he had concluded it, he smiled brightly to himself, for he believed the letter to be one of the best things he had written.

At the barber-shop he passed the solicitous Mr. Clifford and his associates, and climbed to the throne, where he waited.

" Can you tell me about the gentleman in charge of this department? " he asked.

" Pink ! " shouted Mr. Adams.

" Yes, seh ; right heah, seh," came a voice from behind the morning customer, and Pink emerged from the corner pocket, and with his head far back looked at the morning customer from under wavering eyelids.

" You want to keep awake, there," said Mr. Adams very sternly.

" Yes, seh," replied Pink meekly, with a concealed grin. " Good mawnin', misteh."

" Good morning, Mr. Marsh. Have you got time to do a little something to these shoes ? "

" Have I got time ? Well, you know me, misteh. I ain't heah to ovehlook no friend o' mine, no, seh."

He seated himself in front of the shoe on the foot-rest and asked in a low tone : " You heah Misteh Adams make 'at wahm crack at me ? "

" Yes ; he seems to be full of authority this morning."

" All of 'em, misteh ; ev'y one of 'em thinks he 's got to call off f' me, o' else I jus' could n' get along. Misteh Cliffo'd, he 's boss ; Misteh Adams, he 's sup'nten-den'; Misteh Bahclay, he 's manageh, an' 'at new bahbeh, he 's fo'man. Yes, seh ; I 'm wuhkin' faw fo' men heah. Misteh Adams got to get back at somebody 'cuz his wife sutny got him tame down. W'y, Mis' Adams come down heah 'bout twice a week an' shake Misteh Adams down f' ev'y cent he 's got. Yes, seh ; when she gets th'ough 'ith him he 's so clean he don' need to take no bath faw month. Yes, seh; he see huh comin' down 'em staihs an' he kind o' tuhns pale an' stahts in to hunt faw what he's got. She won't even leave him no pinch o' change f' cah faih. He got to touch Misteh Cliffo'd to get home. 'At's a fac'."

"Well, every man likes to give orders to some one."

"Suah thing, misteh. I do n' caih what 'ese bahbehs say to me. I jus' want to stay heah till 'em green leaves come out, an' 'en I'm goin' 'o get a chaih o' my own somewheahs. I sutny do n' like to split my good coin 'ith no white man."

"Well, as I've told you a dozen times, if you want to get into business for yourself, you must begin and save your money."

"Yes, seh; jus' you watch me. If ev'ything comes good, misteh, 'long 'bout nex' August I'll be eatin' watehmelon an' smokin' cigahs when 'em white bahbehs is settin' 'round heah fightin' flies."

"'Hope springs eternal in the human

A LABOR OF LOVE

breast; man never is, but always to be, blest,'" observed the morning customer.

"O, I guess 'at's pooh, ain't it? 'At's bad writin'. Gi' me to me agen, misteh. 'At's one I want to pass to ol' Gawge Lippincott."

"You look it up yourself. You can find it in any book of poetry."

"Hush, man! I know who wrote 'at, an' you can't make me believe nothin' else —no, seh."

"Well, who wrote it?"

"Misteh, I know who done it. You done it, yo'se'f—ain't 'at so?"

"How did you suspect it?" asked the morning customer, laughing.

"Misteh, you can't fool me all 'e time. On'y man could do it. What is it— 'Hope in 'e human breast'? Goodness, if I could jus' toss off few like 'at I'd have some of 'em State Street rascals jumpin' out of 'e windows."

"Speaking of your social affiliations,

have you succeeded as yet in effecting a reconciliation with Miss Jackson?"

Pink looked up, and his big eyes were blinking gravely. But the morning customer kept a straight face. It served his purpose to remain calm and unconcerned when he was hurling these big words.

Pink chuckled away down in his lungs as he folded the flannel.

" 'At Miss Lo'ena Jackson use me jus' like man she neveh seen. I passed huh on 'e street otheh day, an' she begin' lookin' f' some one at secon' sto'y window. She kep' lookin' at 'e window, an' neveh see me at all—jus' gi' me 'at ' brush-by ' sign, an' no mo'. When it comes to playin' faw huh, misteh, I 'm jus' a deuce in a duhty deck—'at 's all."

" Do you think you could reinstate yourself in her affections if you were to write to her? "

" Misteh, she 's keen. Yes, seh, she 's took a lot of 'at co'n f'om 'em cullud boys,

an' she's beginnin' to give ev'y man 'at
bad look when he tells huh how good she
is. Misteh, you can't feed it to 'em f'-
eveh. No, seh, 'ey sutny get wise afteh
while."

" Did n't you say you wanted me to get
up a letter to send to her? "

" Misteh, I tell you one thing—if I eveh
land 'at baby back on 'e resehvation I jus'
got to have one of 'em wahm lettehs like
you sent to Misteh Cliffo'd. No talk 'at I
can swing is eveh goin' 'o move 'at lady;
no, seh."

" Well, I 'll tell you, Pink, I have con-
cocted an epistle here which may act as a
solvent on her heart. I 'll read it to you,
and if you think it 's all right, you can
send it."

" All right, misteh? All right? It jus'
could n' he'p but be all right. Watch out
faw 'em white bahbehs. If 'ey see you
readin' 'at, ev'y one of 'em 's goin' 'o rubbeh, suah."

" You do n't want them to hear it, eh? "

" Goodness, misteh!   I should say not.
I got trouble 'nough heah now 'ithout
havin' all 'ese smaht boys askin' me 'bout
'at guhl ev'y ten minutes."

" All right.   I 'll read it low.   Are you
ready? "

" Misteh, I can't heah it too soon."

The morning customer made sure that
the barbers were out of hearing distance.
They were bunched at the other end of
the room, talking about things to eat.

He leaned over and read, and during
the reading Pink was so absorbed that he
simply rubbed the shoe in a slow and
absent-minded way.

" To Miss Jackson, the Hebe of her Sex.

" My Dearest Miss Jackson: Seated here to-
day, in my boudoir, my thoughts revert to these
beautiful lines:

" 'You may break, you may shatter
The vase, if you will,
But the scent of the roses
Will cling round it still.'

"OSCAH WELLINGTON"

"You may project me into ethereal space, Miss Jackson, but you cannot induce me to forget those whilom hours when you and I were wont to

"'* * * breathe out the tale
Beneath the milk-white thorn.'

"I have been meditating to-day upon the cruelties of Fate. Only a few days ago we were bound together by the reciprocal bonds of Love's young dream. To-day you scorn the sable Lothario who, figuratively speaking, prostrates himself at the shrine of Beauty and begs the slight meed of forgiveness, even if he can never again bask in the dazzling effulgence of your incandescent society. Something tells me that a dark cloud has come between us. Who can it be that would seek to uproot the budding tendrils of Platonic love and plant in place thereof the noxious weeds of venomous hatred? Surely these words will convey to your susceptible woman's heart some approximate conception of the mental anguish which racks my sturdy frame. The birds, sweet harbingers of spring, will soon be disporting themselves in the trees, ever and anon bursting forth into joyous melody.

" ' Come, gentle spring,
    Ethereal mildness, come.'

" In fancy I had pictured many glad days
during this period of the earth's awakening. I
had thought that we would go forth beside the
babbling brook and listen to the soughing wind
whisper its message to our eager souls. I
await a token which will bring me, palpita-
ting with love, to make amends for all the sad
and bitter past. I beg to subscribe myself,
very apologetically,"

Pink made motions with his hands, as
if he were recovering consciousness.

" 'At 's 'e wahmest eveh!' he exclaimed.
" Misteh, you send 'at to Miss Lo'ena
Jackson an' she 'll be wuhkin' on it a yeah
f'om now. Yes, seh, she 'll be settin' up
nights spellin' out 'em long ones."

" You will observe that I said nothing
about your being intoxicated on the night
when you should have taken her to the
party," said the morning customer, folding
the letter.

" O, I guess you ain't wise, neetheh!

PINK MARSH

Misteh, I neveh could n' 'splain to huh 'bout 'at night I got good on gin an' honey. You done right. Jus' let 'at go. Wait 'll she gets 'at letteh. My goodness, misteh! She'll be waitin' out on 'em cah tracks faw me to get home."

Pink took hold of the letter as if it were an explosive. He promised to mail it immediately.

"Misteh, I'm a good ol wagon, but I done broke down, jus' like it says in 'at song," began Pink Marsh.

"What's the matter now?"

"You know 'at lettch you got up faw me to sen' to Miss Lo'ena Jackson."

"Yes. Did you send it?"

"'At's what I done, misteh, an' it was too good. Yes, seh, it was so high she could n' reach it."

"You seemed to think that letter was going to placate her."

"Yes, seh, I kind o' s'posed she 'uz wahm enough to 'peciate suah-thing letteh, but I'm tellin' you she do n' know yet what 'at letteh's about. I'm done 'ith 'at lady. She mus' n' come neah me no mo'. I

GRANT WILLIAMS

jus' hope huh an' 'at Gawge Lippincott gets mah'ied, 'cuz I can see him out stealin' coal right now. 'At Gawge Lippincott wants to keep in nights, too, misteh. Ev'y night he wants to lock 'e dooh an' go to bed, 'cuz I tell you he ain't safe. If he eveh gets on 'e same street 'ith me, I 'm li'ble to cloud up an' rain on him. Yes, seh, people be pickin' up dahk meat all oveh 'e South Side."

" Well, well, you are warlike this morning."

" He 's 'e one 'at done it, misteh. He tol' huh ev'ything he knows 'bout me. Yes, seh, he 's been knockin' good an' plenty, an' if he ain't caihful I 'll fly down an' bite a piece out o' him. When I get th'ough 'ith him, people come up an' say, ' My goodness, 'at ain't Gawge Lippincott,' an' 'en 'ey all go to lookin' faw his face."

" Well, I hope it will not be as serious as that," said the morning customer.

"What's the matter? Did n't the girl answer the letter?"

"Yes, seh, misteh; she sent answeh, an' she did n' do thing to Misteh William Pinckney Mahsh, neetheh. W'y, misteh, I could read Gawge Lippincott in 'at letteh jus' same as if his pickchah on it. Yes, seh, misteh, 'ey 'll be a fune'al on Ahmoh Av'nue, an' ol' Gawge Lippincott won't heah no music. 'At 's right, seh. I 'm a man among men, an' when any punkin-cullud houn' goes suhculatin' 'roun' spoilin' my cha'cteh, his friends want to begin speakin' faw caih'ages right away, 'cuz 'ey got to make a trip to 'at graveyahd, suah."

"What did she say in the letter?"

Pink turned around to see if the white barbers were watching him, and then he drew a crumpled envelope from his hip pocket and passed it up to the morning customer.

The letter had been written with pencil and was blurred and smeary, but the morning customer made it out to be as follows :

" Mr. Marsh, Esq. Dear Sir: Probly you think you can cause me to feel diferent about the eve when you was to be my company at the ball which is not so. Oh I think you had better try to write one more letter and then stop it is not because I wanted to go with you as it is not the case you know that I have gentelmen friends who do not get so drunk when they are to take you that evry one hears about it Ha, Ha, so you see.I know a sertain persen said Oh why do you waist a 2 cent stamp on him but I said to let him know he ain't so smart after all. Yours truely,

"Lorena Jackson."

When the morning customer had finished reading, he shook his head, choked down an inclination to laugh, and said : " Well, Pink, she is certainly a wonder."

Pink looked up and caught the morning customer grinning, and then he began to laugh.

" Misteh, 'at guhl ain' got no mo'

ej'cation 'an 'at stove oveh theah," he said. "She can jus' put on one of 'em regulah Mis' Potteh Palmeh fronts when it comes to settin' up an' talkin', but when you make huh put it down on papeh, w'y, you got 'uh lost, suah. 'Em wuhds ain't right, ah they, misteh?"

"Some of them might be improved upon."

"Look at 'at letteh! Looks like some one been th'owin' coal dust at 'e papeh."

"She certainly conveys the impression that you are *persona non grata*."

"O, man! 'At's a new one, suah! 'At's faw'eign, ain't it? Wha''s 'e defmition?"

"Well, it means that you 're not in it."

"'At's right, misteh. I might jus' well teah up my tickets now, but I 'm goin' o' be good loseh. I make no holleh, misteh. She 'uz neveh mo 'n thuhty to one shot noways, an' I on'y played couple o' dollahs on 'uh."

" You never gave her that bicycle you promised, then, did you ? "

Pink stopped work and spluttered with mirth. Then he said : " Misteh, it ain' no good way to do. It ain't right to fool 'em 'at way, no, seh. Lo'ena lose huh wheel now, suah. I 'll have to use 'at bike sto'y on some otheh lady. Lo'ena ain't 'e on'y good thing on Deahbohn Street. 'Ey 'll be many a wahm child standin' at 'e front gate an' waitin' f' Misteh Mahsh nex' summeh. I 'm like 'at boy in 'e oct'oon show. ' All coons looks alike to me.' "

" Oh, yes, that 's a song. I think I 've heard it."

" Yes, an' 'at 's a pooh one, too. 'At 's bad. Le's see—' O, all '—no, 'at 's too high. ' All coons looks '—'at 's 'bout right."

With his eyes dreamily half-closed, Pink sang as follows, using the soft pedal :

" All a-coons looks alike to me;
I got a new beau, you see,

An' he 's-a jus' as good to me
As you, niggeh, eveh daihed to be,
He 's sutny a-good to me;
He spen's his-a money free.
I do n' like you a-nohow ;
All-a coons looks alike to me."

" You have quite a voice," said the morning customer.

" Hush, misteh, you did n' know I belong to 'at Elect'ic Quahtette. My goodness ! Me an' Grant Williams an' Oscah Wellington an' Fred Bahnett. Oh-h-h, when we hit 'at sassy chohd in ' Ev'nin' by Moonlight,' wheah it comes, ''Ey would set all night an' listen-n-n-n '—I guess 'at 's bad. We get in a minoh 'at 'd coax a buhd out of a cage. You ought to see Fred use 'at guitah. Yes, seh, he sutny does things to it. Yes, seh, we sung in 'e campaign—on'y one night we got too fah west. Cullud man got no business goin' on otheh side of 'e riveh. We all went oveh to meetin' on 'e Wes' Side an' sing

'em wahm 'publican songs, an' we 'uz
good. We did n' think it, misteh—we
knowed it. We knowed 'ey wuz none
betteh. Jus' we come out, misteh, bing!
brickbat right th'ough ol' Fred Bahnett's
guitah. Mo 'n a thousan' I'ishmen afteh
us, misteh; 'at 's right. You talk 'bout
cullud men havin' bad feet; you ought to
see us run 'at night—Mahsh in 'e lead,
Wellington close secon', Williams and
Bahnett neck-an'-neck, two lengths behind. We broke all recohds—we had to
do it. You think 'ey eveh get us back
on 'e Wes' Side? Huh-uh! We know
ouah business."

" You 've got as much right over there
as any one has."

" Co'se! Suah! But we ain' goin'
oveh no mo' when 'em people 's all het up
'bout pol'tics. 'At 's like 'e cullud man
oveh in 'e jail. His lawyeh comes in to
see him, an' he says to 'e cullud man,
' 'Ey can't put you in jail faw what you

done,' an' 'e cullud man says, ' I know 'ey can't, Misteh Lawyeh, but I'm in heah jus' 'e same.' 'At's 'e way 'ith us, misteh. We got mo' rights 'an anybody, but it sutny ain't safe to use 'em."

"GAWGE"

On Independence in Politics

About a week after the morning customer had read the letter from Miss Lorena Jackson, he made another visit to Mr.
Clifford's shop.   Pink was very happy
and explained that as soon as he had paid
off a few small debts he expected to open
an account in a savings bank.   When he
had finished cleaning the morning customer's shoes, preparatory to spreading the
first layer of dressing, a tall negro came
down the stairway and put his head in at
the door.

" Misteh Mahsh heah ? " he asked.

Mr. Clifford, the potentate of the shop,
was rubbing a quinine tonic into the thin
fuzz belonging to a fat man whose jowls
lapped down on the napkin and whose
eyes were wide open from the zest of the

occasion. At brief intervals he groaned
with enjoyment, for it is a fact that having
one's head rubbed is a pure and noble
pleasure on which the gods have set no
high price. Between these groans the fat
man advanced his views on the subject of
tariff legislation. Every opinion was
warmly seconded by Mr. Clifford, who
was fully able to think tariff and rub the
fat man's head, both at the same time.

The interruption of the tariff discussion
seemed to annoy Mr. Clifford. He did
not condescend to answer the question put
to him. He simply made an inclination
of the head toward the remote corner in
which Pink and the morning customer
were having their quiet session.

" Good mawning, Pink," said the visitor,
advancing briskly, and trailing a small
bamboo cane on the floor.

" How do, Gawge," replied Pink, as he
looked up at the visitor, and then, through
some mysterious influence which directs

the happiness of Afro-American souls, both of them began to shake with laughter.

The so-called "Gawge" was rather tan-colored. A small allotment of freckles gave his face a rusty tinge, while the kinks of his hair and mustache were touched with auburn. He wore a high stiff hat with a narrow rim, a suit of navy blue, which had become spotted black here and there by usage, and the morning customer made particular note of his scarfpin, which was a large owl's head, carved of bone and having knobby glass eyes.

"I s'pose you know 'bout ouah goin' to puhfeck an ohganization to-night," said "Gawge."

"'At meetin', you mean?" asked Pink.

"It's 'specially desiahed by Misteh Milleh 'at we get a good 'tendance at Mc-Cahty's Hall to-night. You be suah an' come an' exuht yo' infloonce to get all 'e boys out. It's goin' to be called 'Milleh In'epen'en' Cullud Voters League.' I'm

sec'eta'y, an' nachu'lly I feel 'sponsible.
Misteh Milleh re'lizes ouah infloonce an'
he's goin' to be ve'y lib'al."

" Yes, seh, Gawge, I 'll be on hand."

" Well, I got to be goin' oveh county
buildin' an' see a gem'man. Smoke a
cigah, Pink?"

So saying, " Gawge " drew a very pale
cigar from his pocket and handed it to
Pink, and then he went out, still trailing
his cane over the tiling.

" Who's that — a friend of yours?"
asked the morning customer.

" Who, him? He's 'e boy 'at stahted
pol'tics. He's 'e one 'at says who is an'
who ain't. Did you kind o' notice how
he flash in an' flash out? He knows mo'
'bout pol'tics 'an Gen'al Grant eveh did.
When ol' Gawge dies 'ey won't be no mo'
pol'tics, no seh."

" What's his name?"

" 'At 's 'e on'y Gawge 'at eveh happened — Gawge Lippincott."

"GUS MILLEH"

" George Lippincott ? Why, he's the man you were going to kill, is n' he ? "

" Look at him, misteh. I could n' kill good thing like 'at."

" Why, it was n't a week ago that you told me that the first time you saw him you intended to annihilate him — simply slaughter him in cold blood."

Pink chuckled aloud and wagged his head knowingly. " Mus n' kill Gawge now," he said. " We both eatin' out of 'e same pan, yes, seh. I 'uz goin' 'o do Gawge mo' hahm 'an any man eveh had done to him, but 's no use now, misteh. Gawge is wheah I am now. 'At Lo'ena Jackson toss him a mile higheh 'an she give it to me. She got a new face in 'e pahlah now, suah. Gawge an' me 's shahpenin' razahs on 'e same hone 'iss week. Hen'y Clahk 's 'e man 'at 's got to be took off 'e map. He's 'e hot papa oveh at Lo'ena's house 'iss week."

" Do you mean to say that Mr. Lippincott has received his congé ?"

" No, seh, I do n' know 'bout no con-
jay, but he sutny got 'e mahble h'aht f'om
little Miss Lo'ena. She can' no mo' see
wheah he comes in now an' if he 'd neveh
been. Yes, seh, she fawgets wheah she
met him. She do n't even know his name.
W'y, misteh, if me an' ol' Gawge go up
'e street togetheh an' she meet us, she
say, ' My goodness ! Town 's jus' full o'
strangehs to-day.' 'At 's how well she
likes us, misteh."

" How did Mr. Lippincott happen to
lose his standing?"

" Hen'y Clahk done it. Hen'y 's swell
lookeh an' got a con talk 'at 'd win most
any lady. He 's po'teh on Pullman cah,
an' he jus' land in heah otheh day f'om
long piece o' wuhk in p'ivate cah—been
way out West. You know, misteh, pahty
o' white gem'men out in cah 'at way gen'-
ally ve'y lib'al 'ith a po'teh 'at knows how

to use 'em. I guess Hen'y ain't smooth
o' nothin', neetheh! Goodness, misteh,
he can brush a man an' bow an' say ' Ev'y-
thing sa'sfacto'y, seh?' an' 'e man jus' got
to hand him money. Pahty out two o'
three weeks like 'at, an' when 'ey come in
ev'y gem'man give 'e po'tch much as
five o' ten dollahs 'piece. Ol' Hen'y land
in heah 'ith a roll 'at made me an' Gawge
Lippincott look like a couple o' dahk lob-
stehs. Money in ev'y pocket, misteh;
p'fume'y on his cloze, an' smokin' 'at long
kind 'at you neveh get f' no nickel—no,
seh. He meet Lo'ena an' say, ' Miss
Jackson, may I espec' 'e honah of givin'
you some soda-wateh? ' o' someping like 'at,
an' 'en he flash 'at bundle o' papeh money.
Oh-h-h-h, I guess not! I s'pose she did n'
nail him! Wha' d' you s'pose, misteh?
Ol' Hen'y loosens up an' buys huh watch.
Gawge Lippincott go 'round 'at ev'nin' to
see huh, an' she send out wuhd 'at if he
do n' go 'way she'll set 'e dogs on him.

Gawge can feed 'em nice talk, misteh, but he sutny went into 'e fence soon as Hen'y showed up an' begin to make good 'ith his coin. Lo'ena 's like all of 'em, misteh; she 's lookin' faw 'e boy 'at 'll let go f' theatchs an' jew'lery. When Hen'y give up 'at gol' watch, 'at 'uz when Gawge Lippincott splosh into 'e mud. He 'll luhn, misteh, he 'll luhn. I 'm jus' waitin' faw Hen'y Clahk's finish now. Jus' soon as he uses las' strippeh of 'at roll an' do n' put up nothin' 'cept sayin' how he loves huh, she 'll find out 'at he ain't propeh comp'ny, an' ol' Hen'y 'll be out on 'e road makin' up loweh seven and guessin' why."

" I 'm afraid you 're a pessimist as regards the gentle sex."

" I 'm wuhse 'an 'at, misteh. I 'm an Ind'an on 'iss heah guhl game. I won't stan' f' nothin' no mo'."

" Well, I must say that you and Mr. Lippincott are bearing up very bravely under your affliction. Mr. Lippincott seems to be finding surcease from his grief in the exciting field of politics."

" Misteh, I wish you 'd used someping like 'at when Gawge 'uz in heah. Gawge thinks he 's ve'y strong on 'em big wuhds, an' I jus' like to steeh him 'genst some one 'at could make him look foolish. Did you heah 'e kind he 'uz passin' to me in heah? "

" Yes, he seemed to be quite a talker."

" He 's a wahm talkeh, an' 'at 's all he can do, misteh. Gawge thinks he 's 'e whole thing in pol'tics out in ouah wahd, an' nobody likes to wake him up. He 's goin' 'o make Gus Milleh aldehman — 'at 's what he told Misteh Milleh, an' Misteh Milleh he thinks 'at Gawge got 'e whole cullud vote inside of 'at blue vest. I know betteh. If Gus Milleh wants to land me he betteh come an' see me himse'f. What he does faw ol' Gawge Lippincott ain't helpin' me none—no, seh.

Cullud man's 'e real thing 'long 'bout spring 'lection, an' any man 'at gets me to holle'in' faw him has sutny got to use me good. Gawge Lippincott do n't own nobody but himse'f. I 'll smoke ol' Gawge's cigars 'at Gus Milleh pays faw, but when it comes to castin' my ballot, seh, as an Ameh'can cit'zen, Gawge Lippincott an' no otheh cullud man goin' 'o tell me how to vote—no, seh. I 'm faw any man 'at does 'e most faw me—yes, seh."

On the Selection of Apparel

" O, man ! I guess you picked 'at out o'
some ash-bah'el! " exclaimed Pink Marsh
as the morning customer seated himself on
the throne and spread the new spring overcoat so that he would not sit on it.

" What are you talking about ? O,
I see — the coat. Is it all right ? "

" No, seh, it 's bad — all ragged 'roun'
'e edges, do n't fit in back. 'At 's a pooh
coat. Goodness ! Do n' eveh take it off
when yo' in heah, 'cuz if you do, you lose
it to me. I jus' need one of 'em shawt
cream-cullud boys to make me good. I
do n't steal, misteh, but I sutny could use
'at coat."

" Well, I 'm glad you like it. It 's
always a satisfaction to have one 's dress

131

approved by a gentleman of taste and discrimination."

" Hush, man, do n't lift me too high. It ain't ev'y cullud boy 'at gets 'at lang'age used on him, is it ? "

" No, sir, that is a special eulogium."

" I jus' see 'at one when it go past me. 'Logeum' — 'logeum' — misteh, you got a new one to toss at me ev'y time you come in heah, an' none of 'em ain't so wuhse. 'At 's a fact, seh. Some is wahmeh 'an othehs, but ev'y one of 'em smokes."

" That is very kind of you to say so."

" I guess you do n' know how to use cullud pusson good, neetheh. W'y, misteh, some days afteh you come in heah an' give me 'at kind o' convehsation, I feel 'at if I had mo' ej'cation I would n' be rubbin' no man's shoes, no, seh. I 'd be lawyeh o' someping like 'at."

" Well, do n't you worry too much. You 're probably doing more business than half of the lawyers."

"'LONZO"

" 'At 's all right, mistch, but I 'd like to be one of 'em boys 'at gets up an' says, ' Misteh judge an' gem'men of 'iss ju'y, it is p'ivilege faw me to 'peciate yo' 'tention in regahds to 'iss subjec' an' to—"

" Well, do n't forget that you are supposed to be shining those shoes," said the morning customer.

Pink had become so interested in his majestic impersonation of the lawyer addressing the jury that he had laid down his brushes, put one hand on his chest, and extended the other in a sweeping gesture.

When the morning customer interrupted his speech, he suddenly collapsed into laughter and rocked about on his stool, until the morning customer, who seldom gave way to mirth, began to chuckle out of sympathy.

Pink returned to his work on the shoe, but he was still seized with occasional spasms of laughter, and the big yellow-white balls of his eyes were wet with genuine tears.

"It's rather warm in here this morning," observed the morning customer, after Pink had simmered down to his normal gravity, "but I'm afraid to take off this coat after what you said."

"It's all right if you watch it, misteh, but you sutny mus' watch it. I on'y got one kick comin' on 'at coat, misteh."

"Yes — and what's that?"

"Yes, seh, if yo' goin' 'o kill 'em dead, you ought to have some of 'at satin down 'e front. 'Lonzo Williams, down on Twent'-sevem Street, got one of 'em satin kind, so wahm it melts snow right off 'e sidewalk when 'e walks past. People got to put on 'em smoked glasses to look at ol' 'Lonzo when he comes out 'ith 'at coat, suah. Yes, seh, it's kind o' cullah of cana'y buhd, all 'cept down 'e front, an' theah it's blue satin. Oh-h-h-h, I guess it ain't wahm o' nothin'! Got puhl but-

tons 'bout 'e size of five-cent pie. 'Lonzo
come 'long Ahmoh Av'nue 'ith 'at coat on,
an' you see 'em, old an' young, misteh,
leavin' theah homes to follow him.   Yes,
seh, he got to tuhn 'round an' yell at 'em
to make 'em go back in 'e houses and
leave him alone.   Yes, seh, ol' 'Lonzo
put 'e price o' many a shave into 'at
coat."

" Why don't you get one like it, if it
gives a man such a standing ? "

" My goodness, misteh! 'em coats do n'
grow on bushes.   No, seh, you sutny got
to wave money in front of a tailah befo' he
hands you anything like 'at.   W'y do n't
I get one !   I can jus' answeh questions
like 'at all day.   Ask me some mo'.   Ask
me why I do n' buy 'at Lake-Front Pahk
an' move it out on Deahbohn Street.
Misteh, I could n' even buy one of 'em
sassy buttons."

" Well, you know what I 've been telling you for three months.   Save your

money. Put away a little something every week, and you 'll be surprised to find how it accumulates."

" 'At 's no lie, misteh, what you tellin' me now. I 'll be sup'ised, suah 'nough, if I eveh find any money 'cumulatin' in my cloze. I thought Misteh McKinley get in down at Washin'ton kind o' move mattehs some — kind o' push a little coin towahds me, but do n' seem to, seh."

" Well, of course, if you go and play your money against policy, McKinley can't help you any. What did you count on ? Did you think that after McKinley got in he 'd send you some money every week ? The only way in which McKinley could help you would be to come here and have his shoes shined."

" Well, co'se, misteh, I did n' 'spect to get anything 'less I went out faw it, but I 'uz hopin' I 'd have mo' luck afteh Misteh McKinley got to be presiden'."

" Yes, you probably thought he might

"WAHMEST EVEH"

help you catch something at policy. Suppose you aid win twenty, thirty, or even fifty dollars at policy. What good would it do you? You'd go out to spend the money, and the chances are that you'd lose your job here. Then where would you be? You'd be out of money and out of a job. I suppose you'd come around to me again and want me to write another letter to Mr. Clifford to get you back into this job."

Pink listened seriously enough until the morning customer had concluded, and then he shook his head and gave way to internal laughter. He made no sound, but his shoulders lifted now and then. He looked up at the morning customer with a moist grin, and said: "No, seh, I fool you, misteh. I would n' waste no good coin on 'em cullud people no mo'. No, seh; I take 'at money an' I make myse'f good. —'at's what I'd do. See heah, misteh— one o' 'em stiff white hats 'ith a soft top,

kind o' pushed in, an' black band 'round
it, un'e'stand! Co'se I would n' have no
patent-leatheh shoes—I s'pose not. 'Ese
shahp boys, 'ith yellow tops. Pants—kind
o' buff-cullud. Coat! O, say, misteh,
I do n' s'pose I'd have one 'ith stripes,
would I? No braid 'long edges, neetheh.
O, man! I'd be 'e wahmes' thing 'at
eveh come up undeh 'at Twelf' Street
vi'duc'. I would 'n do thing but jus' walk
up an' down in front o' Miss Lo'ena
Jackson's house an' say: 'Woman, see
what you missed.'"

"You'd have to get a cane with a
silver dog's-head, would n't you?" suggested the morning customer.

"I'm buyin' it now, misteh; I'm buyin'
it now."

"And a white silk cravat with gold
horseshoe on it!"

"Misteh, you sutny got to stop 'at; I
can't see yo' shoe."

"Then you want a diamond ring and a

double watch-chain with a cameo charm,
and a spotted handkerchief with musk on
it, and a pair of yellow gloves and—"

" Man alive ! Do n' say no mo'! I 'm
so dopey now I can't finish yo' shoe. You
sutny got to stop."

" How about smoking a ten-cent cigar ?"

" Make it fifteen, misteh, 'ith a yellow
papeh 'round it. Put about fo' hund'ehd
dollahs in my cloze while yo' at it. Goodness, I sutny am havin' good time to-day."

When the morning customer went
away, Pink was just as happy as though he
had bought the clothes.

On the Transference of Affections

The morning customer had heard of men losing weight and drooping away to melancholy through disappointment in love, but he observed that Pink was too much of a philosopher to keep company with grief. The boy gave up Lorena Jackson with no sigh of regret. He no longer talked of her.

One day the morning customer, who wished to learn if Pink had a secret sorrow, said in the most casual way :

" I have n't heard you speak of your lady friend lately."

" She ain' no frien' o' mine no mo'— 'at lady, you mean. Some day when she 's washin' faw livin' to keep some cheap cullud hound in smokin'-tobacco, you see

PINK MARSH

Misteh William Pinckney Mahsh takin' his
wash 'roun' to huh an' say : ' Woman, if
you do n' get 'iss bundle ready by to-moh'ow
night, I take my wuhk somewheahs else,
an' you all stahve to death.' Yes, seh,
I 'll see 'e day, misteh, when 'at piece o'
p'oud flesh 'll be doin' up my collahs faw
me."

" You should n't be so bitter. You
seemed to think at one time that Miss—
what 's her name ? "

" Miss Lo'ena Jackson, yes seh."

" Well, you seemed to think at one
time that Miss Jackson was an amphibious
sort of a girl."

" Misteh, I seen a new stah in 'e sky,
an' it shines brighteh an' eveh you see 'at
ninety-poun' lady. Le' me tell you,
misteh. She ain't so 'phibious as some
othehs. 'Ey 's a big crop of 'em on 'e
South Side, an' if you lose one you suah
find anotheh waitin' faw you 'round 'e
cawneh."

" I see—just as good fish in the sea as ever were caught."

" Jus' as good fish, misteh, but you sutny do need a little bait. 'Ey won' bite at no baih hook. Yes, seh, you can ketch tuhtle 'ith a piece o' string, misteh, but you got to use fresh bait to land a goggle-eye. An' you got to pull when 'at cohk goes undeh, o' little Miss Goggle-Eye up stream an' took yo' bait 'long 'ith huh."

" Well, you are decidedly figurative this morning."

" 'At 's so, misteh, I got it all figgahed out. Man get stung three o' fo' times an' he gets wiseh, no mistake, seh. I 'm lookin' f' no mo' ladies 'at 's aftch bikes. I 'm wantin' 'em, misteh, 'at if you give 'em a few peppehmints an' stan' faw cah-faih, 'ey think they bein' used good. Yes, seh. I kind o' got one snaihed out now, an' I sutny won't spoil 'uh by talkin' jew'lery to 'uh, cuz when you staht 'em in

strong you got to make good all 'e time, o'
you come to bad finish."

" You've given up all hopes of reconciliation with Lorena, then, have you?"

" Misteh, 'at lady's jus' 'e same to me
as day befo' yes'day. She could n' coax
me back to huh, even if she use sugah."

" How about chicken? Suppose she
invited you over to her house to eat
chicken?"

" Misteh, I might fool 'ith any chicken
she set out," and Pink shook with laughter; " but she could n' neveh tie me down
in 'at pa'lah agen, faw I'm tellin' you I
know all 'bout 'at lady's style. You know
what she done to Hen'y Clahk? I tol'
you 'bout Hen'y Clahk, did n' I?"

" Is he the Pullman porter that cut you
and George Lippincott out?"

" Yes, seh, 'at's 'e one. You know
he loosen up an' buy 'at gold watch faw
Lo'ena. He 'uz 'e hot papa f' 'bout two
weeks, an' 'en he went broke. Afteh 'at

he begin usin' talk on huh same as ol'
Gawge Lippincott. Jus' soon as Hen'y
could n' p'oduce no mo', she find out 'at
he 's tellin' bad sto'ies 'bout huh cha'cteh,
an' she goin' 'o have him cahved by light
fellow 'at wihks in a club. When ol'
Hen'y went back on his cah he uz stripped
so clean he could n' change dollah faw
man 'at wanted to give him quahteh.
'At 's what 'at long-waisted fai'y done to
Hen'y Clahk. Misteh, she 's sutny a
quick finisheh. I 'm 'bout 'e on'y boy
she neveh sunk 'e hooks into. I kep' huh
guessin' 'bout 'at bisickle she 'uz goin' 'o
get. I s'pose she likes me, do n't she?
She got 'at yellow waiteh now. Yes, seh,
if he gets his pay in aftehnoon, you can
sutny gamble 'at she 's he'pin' him spend
it in 'e ev'nin' —an' any time he 's slow in
comin' up, I can jus' see him huntin' f'
new place."

" Well, do I understand you to say that
you have a new — young lady? "

BELLE

" Mistch, I can't say I got huh faw suah, becuz I get 'at con so often befo' 'at I'm slow to say what's mine till 'e race is oveh an' all tickets paid, but it sutny looks as if 'at Miss Belle Hopkins jus' look all 'round an' 'en could n' see nobody else but Misteh William Pinckney Mahsh. She's whispehed it to me, mistch, 'at if she lose me, ev'ything sutny off, but ol' Misteh Wise Pink, he's huhd 'at talk befo'. I ain't makin' no claims, mistch, 'til I see somebody try to land huh 'way f'om me. 'En I can tell if she's goin 'o stick. Any hoss can win, mistch, if he's got 'e track to himse'f, but you bring out ol' hoss numbeh two, an' 'e one 'at picks 'em up oftenes' an' sets 'em down fah apaht is 'e one 'at you want to put yo' money on."

" What kind of a looking girl is Belle? "

" Betteh 'n 'at, mistch. She's betteh 'n yo' guessin' she is. Yes, seh, she's got mo' feathehs 'an any otheh blackbuhd 'at eveh flew 'long Deahbohn Street, an' she

got mo' style in huh walk in one minute
'an 'at half-stahved Lo'ena Jackson eveh
had in all huh life. My goodness, misteh,
Belle walk jus' like she 'uz takin' last
chance at 'e cake, an' had a bad lady to
beat out. She's win in mo' n' one walk,
an' she'd be on 'e stage walkin' long befo'
'iss, on'y huh motheh's ve'y strong Meth'-
dis' an' do n' like none of 'em pasamala
steps. No, seh, Belle can't do none of 'at
' hand on yo' head an' let yo' mind go free'
while Mis' Hopkins 'round. Mis' Hopkins got mo' 'ligion 'an she can use. I 'uz
down at 'e house otheh ev'nin', an' ol'
Mamma Hopkins she kind o' sized me
oveh 'e tops of 'em specticles, an' say:
' Misteh Mahsh, do you 'tend chuhch?'
I say: ' Yes, umdeed, Mis' Hopkins; I
jus' soon think o' losin' a meal as oveh-
lookin' suhvis.' 'En she say: ' What
chuhch do you 'tend, Misteh Mahsh?' an'
I say, ' I go out Thuhty-fift' Street, 'cuz
'e preacheh out theah most sutny preach

wahm suhmon.' She kind o' look at me an'
shake 'uh head. Yes, seh, I'll have to
holleh some night befo' I'm strong 'ith ol'
Mis' Hopkins. I'll jus' have to go down
to 'at chuhch an' drown out Misteh
Preacheh Fehguson befo' Mis' Hopkins
eveh believe I got 'ligion."

"Yes, Pink, I suppose you are going to
add hypocrisy to your other sins," said the
morning customer.

"No, seh, misteh, 'at ain' no 'poc'asy.
I get comvuhted ev'y time I go to chuhch,
but on week-days I sutny is what Brotheh
Fehguson call a wande'in' sheep. I sutny
wandeh when I get 'way wheah I can't
heah 'at music."

"Well, perhaps Belle will convert
you."

"Hush, man! 'At Belle's a hot tomol-
ley. She no mo' got 'at Meth'dis' 'ligion
'an you have — no, seh. She'd ratheh
push huh feet oveh floo' 'at had sand on
it. She's got bad feet. She do n' know

what to do 'ith 'em feet at all. Shall I kind o' touch up 'at hat, misteh?"

And the morning customer stepped down to be brushed. Pink swung the long and supple broom in fancy curves and beat out fancy time. As the morning customer started toward the door, Pink whispered, "Gawge Lippincott do n' know 'iss guhl at all, an' I 'm sutny goin' 'o keep huh undeh coveh."

On the Relative Value of Education and Wealth

On a bright spring morning, when Pink should have been dwelling on the birth of seasons, he admitted that he was pondering on the benefits of education. Before he spoke, the morning customer noticed that his eyelids were strained, and he whispered to himself.

He worked in silence for several minutes and then consulted the oracle.

"Misteh, I want to ask you q'estion, 'cuz I know you'll tell me right. It's 'bout which is betteh faw you — ej'cation o' money?"

"What got you started on that question?" asked the morning customer.

"Yes, seh, 'ey had a meetin' at 'e F'ed'ick Douglass Club last ev'nin', an' I

went 'ith Gawge Lippincott. 'At's 'e
q'estion 'ey discussed 'bout, which is betteh
faw you to have — ej'cation o' money?"

" Which side did you take?"

" I jus' set theah an' listened to some
of 'em hot boys th'ow lang'age at each
otheh. 'Ey sutny wuz usin' wuhds 'at
neveh 'd been used befo'. I guess it was
pooh, too. Goodness! 'At Gawge Lippincott jus' spread his wings an' sail 'round
an' 'round 'at room like eagle. He neveh
touch flooh at all. You talk 'bout me
bein' in 'at ahgament! W'y, misteh, I
could jus' flutteh a little. I sutny could n'
fly."

" Which side did your friend, Mr. Lippincott, take?"

" Misteh, he could n' see nothin' but
ej'cation. He said 'at a wise boy could
make good even if he did n' have 'e coin,
but if you had all 'e money you could
cah'y an' wuz igno'ant, 'en people would n'
show no manneh o' respec' faw you."

" Yes, but suppose a man has plenty of money — he can travel around the world and employ people to instruct him, and in a little while he will have an education."

" 'At 's so, misteh," said Pink, reflectively. 'At 's ev'y wuhd so, suah 'nough."

" But, on the other hand," said the morning customer, " suppose that a man has education, but no money, to begin with. Can't he use his education to make money? "

" 'At 's what he can do," said Pink, solemnly.

" Suppose he makes money and loses it. He still has his education left, has n't he ? "

" Misteh, you sutny siftin' it. Yes, seh, you sutny gettin' 'at subjec' right up in 'e cawneh so 's it can 't get away f'om you."

" You follow my line of reasoning, do you ? "

" Go on, misteh, I 'm close behind. You can 't lose me."

. " I say, suppose the educated man loses

his money. He still has his education left. But if a man has n't got anything at all but money, and he loses that, where is he ? Tell me that."

" Wheah is he ? Wheah is he, misteh ? W'y, 'at 's his finish, suah. My goodness, misteh, I do wish you 'd been out to 'at F'ed'ick Douglass Club las' night jus' to toss some of 'at kind o' lang'age at some of 'em cullud bladdehs. Ol' Hahvey Wilson 'uz takin' 'e money side, an' he sutny made mo' noise an' done less talkin' an' any man I eveh see. You neveh know what Hahvey 's wantin' to tell you, 'cuz he use 'em wuhds 'at he makes up himself — all 'e time sayin' someping 'bout 'e 'scrambation of illipsical' o' 'ambification faw scientific tomology, an' all 'at. He do n' know what 'at means any mo' 'an you do."

" Well, you know what ' tomology ' means, do n't you ? " asked the morning customer.

"OL' MIS' HOPKINS"

" How 's 'at, misteh? ' Tomology'? "

" Yes, the word ' tomology,' you just used. You know what that means, do n't you? "

Pink rubbed the shoe slowly and appeared to be in deep thought.

" I une'stand in gen'al way e' defimition, but I can 't hahdly tell it."

" ' Tomology' means the science of to-matoes."

" Yes, seh. I knew it 'uz someping like 'at, but Hahvey Wilson, he did n' know, misteh. He jus' huhd somebody use 'at wuhd, an' he say, ' ' At 's a good wuhd. I jus' need 'at ! ' Yes, seh, he thinks 'at ' tomology ' someping about 'e Bible."

" Well, which side won the debate? "

" Misteh, 'at Gawge Lippincott beat Hahvey Wilson at ev'y tuhn in 'e road. My goodness, he had ol' Hahvey hangin' on 'e ropes, but 'ey done him duht, suah. Hahvey got 'at decision. Yes, seh; his brotheh-in-law 'uz one of 'e judges, an'

'notheh judge 'uz Lou Pahkeh 'at Gawge
kep' out o' bein' janitah at 'e police station.
Ol' Gawge sutny had no chance 'genst 'at
push."

" Are you a member of the club ? "

" No, seh; I jus' kind o' follow ol'
Gawge in.   'Bout month ago, misteh, 'ey
sutny had a wahm session 'bout ' Which
is 'e greates', wateh o' fiah ? '   I s'pose
ol' Gawge did n' say a wuhd 'at night.
He jus' ask 'em one q'estion, misteh, 'at
settled 'e whole thing.   He jus' say,
' Wateh can put out fiah, but how 'bout
fiah puttin' out wateh ? ' Afteh he showed
'at wateh 'uz strongeh 'n fiah, he say,
' What 's 'e mos' hahm fiah eveh done ? '
'At 'uz 'e Chicago fiah.   It jus' buhn up
one town, but did n't 'e flood wash away
ev'ything? W'y, misteh, 'at flood wash away
hund'ehds towns 'e size o' Chicago, an'
nobody eveh heah anything mo' 'bout 'em."

" Do you believe that story about
Noah's ark and the flood ? "

" How 's 'at, mistch ? Do I believe 'at sto'y ? Ain't it wrote down in 'e Bible, huh ? "

" Yes, but I did n't know whether you believed it or not."

" Look heah, man ! S'pose I did have some doubts 'bout 'at sto'y. Do n't you think I 'm eveh foolish 'nough to say so. No, seh ; I 'm takin' no chances. I jus' say I b'lieve ev'ything 'at 's put down an' 'en I 'm safe."

" Why, it 's just as bad to have a doubt in your mind as it is to come right out and say so," remarked Mr. Clifford, the head barber, who had lounged over to hear the talk.

" No, seh ! " replied Pink, emphatically. " 'Ey can 't prove nothin' 'genst me if I do n't come out an' say someping. S'pose 'ey say, ' Misteh Mahsh, did you al'uz believe 'e Bible ? ' an' I say, ' Yes, seh.' 'Ey could n' prove what been in my mind; no, seh. Ain' 'at so, misteh ? "

"I'm in doubt about that," said the morning customer.

"But if 'ey say, 'How 'bout 'at mawnin' in 'e bahbeh-shop when you told 'em gem'men 'at you wuz n't suah 'bout Noah an' 'e ahk?'—what could I answeh back? No, seh; you do n't get me into no trouble about 'e Bible. I do n' know what all's in 'at Bible, but I say it's so, o' else it would n't be in. I'm takin' no chances, misteh. I ain' no good chuhch membeh now, but I'm goin' o' keep good on believin' in 'at Bible, so if eveh I get sick o' anything 'e matteh 'ith me, I wont have to squaih myse'f ve'y much. 'At's goin' 'o count faw me, misteh, if I can say I b'lieve 'at Bible all 'e time."

"You have it all figured out," said the morning customer, "and I do n't see how they can lose you."

Pink was much elated to think that he had not been trapped into expressing any doubt as to scriptural revelation.

"PREACHEH FEHGUSON"

On the Sin of Neglecting an Opportunity

The friendship between the morning customer and Pink lasted well, because it was never allowed to drift into familiarity. Whenever the morning customer climbed to the throne, he was greeted with formal politeness. He listened gravely when Pink told his secrets, and, by fine tact, invited confidence even while repelling intimacy. He seldom spoke of himself, and there never can be a real companionship between two persons until they have compared experiences.

After the months had passed, Pink knew the morning customer as an exalted and dignified personage who had command of the wisdom of all ages and allowed his light to shine. And that was all he knew.

The morning customer, on the other hand, knew Pink's biography—the boy's early life in an Ohio town, how he followed the race horses to Chicago, why he gave up working in a dairy lunchroom, and so on, up to the time when he took the room at Mrs. Willard's house and was placed in charge of the boot-polishing department in Mr. Clifford's shop.

It has already appeared that he learned of Pink's habits, his falling from grace, and his recovery of the high intentions to be important and have money of his own. With each visit the morning customer learned something more regarding the boy. For instance, one morning the conversation turned upon the subject of dramatic art, and Pink gave the opinion that "Camille" was the greatest play ever written.

"Took a guhl to see 'at 'Camille' one night," he said. "She jus' shiveh an' hang on to me all 'e way home. I got puhty well roused myse'f."

PINK MARSH

At another time, soon after Pink had expressed his entire faith in the Bible (as set forth in the preceding chapter), he talked of music, and said that " rag-time " melodies pleased him, but that he dared not listen to them during business hours, because the mists came before his eyes and he became so excited that he could not shine shoes. He told of his belief that the angels in heaven played " rag-time " music, and he regarded this as an inducement for all colored people to lead pure lives.

While they were talking of " rag-time " music, the morning customer asked why it was that a colored man could dance so much better than a white man. Pink advanced the explanation that the colored man had fewer bones than the white man, and had his joints peculiarly constructed, according to an all-wise plan. He also held that the white men's bones were " brickle," while the colored man could bend his frame and assume certain shapes which added to the charm of his performance as a dancer. The morning customer shook his head in doubt, and Pink said that a doctor had once explained to him the construction of a colored man, telling him, among other things, that the skull was an inch thick and that the only tender part of the anatomy was the shin-bone.

It happened that just after Pink had won his point concerning the bony structure of the members of his race, two barbers and a man in the second chair became involved in loud talk about the continuous war-cloud in Europe. This interruption gave the morning customer a chance to retire gracefully from the dispute as to anatomy, so he asked:

" Have you been reading the war news in the papers ? "

" Misteh, I got no time faw 'at wah when 'ey 's fo' tracks runnin'; no, seh. I been too busy watchin' 'em at Memphis

"COME AN' TAKE MY MONEY"

to know 'bout 'at wah. I mahked 'em yes'day, mistch, an' three out o' fo' win. an' I did n' have a cent on one of 'em.

" I understand. You 've been making these mind bets — figuring how much you might have won."

" Mistch, I ought to be cah'yin' roll to-day 'at 'd look like bolt o' wall-papeh. " Yes, seh, I had ol' Domingo at Memphis, an' 'at Pahson at Newpoht. Cullud boy tol' me to be suah an' get someping on Pahson as soon as he 'uz good odds. Yes'day, mistch, he 'uz six to one, an' I know he could n' lose, an' heah I set rubbing up tans faw nasty ol' ten a throw when I ought to been oveh in' at back room playin' my cloze on 'at Pahson. W'y, misteh, he went past 'em jus' like 'ey was tied. I know wheah I could got five dollahs yes'day, too. I take 'at five and play Domingo an' Pahson, an' I get mo' 'an hund'ehd of 'em big smiling dollahs to-day."

"I'm afraid I'll never cure you of gambling."

"W'y, misteh, when you see on 'e blackboahd 'at Pahson 's six to one, an' you know he can't lose, I'm tellin' you, misteh, it ain' right to keep 'at money in yo' pocket. If 'at bookmakeh say, 'Come an' take my money,' yo' sutny foolish if you do n' do it."

"I can't see that you've ruined very many bookmakers. Where's all the money you've won on the races?"

"Hush, man! I do n' s'pose I done a thing to ol' Sly Libson one day, did I? I jus' caught 'at rascal seven to one, an' I come back f'om 'e pahk in open caih'age smokin' one of 'em pooh fifteen-cent cigahs."

"Yes, you told me about that. You went out that night and lost your job. How long did your money last you?"

"Neveh mind 'bout 'at time, misteh. Nex' time Misteh Mahsh gets on one of

'em good things, he's goin' 'o take 'at
money an plant it deep, suah."

" What! Are you going to save money
at last?"

" 'At's what I need, misteh. 'At's
what I got to have."

" Well, that's a virtuous resolution,
certainly, but I don't think you'll ever
make any money playing the races."

" You can't tell, misteh. I been feelin' ve'y lucky for sev'al days."

" Well, I hope you'll not be disap-
pointed. Since when have you had this
desire to save money?"

" Well, misteh, you got to have a little,
o' they sutny got no use faw you."

" Who has n't any use for you? I wonder if you are contemplating matrimony."

" Hush, man!"

" What's her name — the new one?"

" Who? 'At Miss Belle Hopkins? I
neveh say I'uz goin' 'o join up 'ith 'at
lady."

" No, but I 'm very suspicious."

Pink laughed away down in his throat, and shook his head warningly. " I do n' say I will mah'y 'at lady, an' I do n' say I won't do it. She 's a cana'y buhd, mis- teh, an' she sings sweet song, but 'e cullud boy ain' got no cage. You can't neveh live on 'em cake-walks. Cake-walks is good, misteh, but you can't eat 'em, no seh! 'At 's ev'y wuhd so. Thank you, seh. How 's 'at, misteh? Keep 'e change? Oh, I s'pose I do n' know how, do I? I tol' you, misteh, 'at I wuz feelin' lucky."

On Secret Defamation of Character

There was a dark cloud in the sky.

Pink Marsh told the morning customer about it at the first opportunity. He began by saying that he would have to write another letter.

"What's the matter?" asked the morning customer.

"Dahk cloud in 'e sky, misteh. Yes, seh, 'ey's a dahk cloud in 'e sky, caused by some low-down cullud pusson, who I call a snake-in-'e-grass right to his ve'y face."

"Who is the snake-in-the-grass?"

"'At's what I can't find out, misteh."

"Well, how can you tell him anything to his face, then?"

" Jus' le' me know who it is, misteh;
'at's all Misteh Mahsh caihs to know.
Yes, seh, he be layin' in 'at shiny box 'an
people go by an' say: ' Jus' looks like
he's 'sleep, do n't he ? ' Co'se, his cloze
goin' 'o coveh up all 'em holes I cahve in
him. I 'm goin' 'o leave 'nough o' him
to make a good fune'al, an' 'at 's 'bout all.

" It is n't George this time — George,
what 's his name ? "

" No, seh, it ain't Gawge. I can't find
out who done it, but if I look in ev'y
house on Deahbohn St'eet, I 'm suah to
find him some time o' otheh, an' when I
do — hush man ! You jus' listen on 'e
Nawth Side, an' you heah him squawk out
Twent'-Sevem Street. Yes, seh, yo'
next."

The last was addressed to a young man
in checked clothes, who had edged up and
was listening with a steadfast grin.

" Who 's that you 're goin' to do up ? "
he asked.

" 'At 's nobody, misteh," replied Pink,
with an averted wink at the morning customer. "I would n' huht nobody. You
jus' have a good chaih, misteh, an' I 'll
sutny use you right in ve'y few minutes.
Heah 's mawnin' papeh, seh, 'at 's got all
'bout 'at Cong'ess. Yes, seh, you get
oveh by 'e window yo' suah to get plenty
o' light. Yes, seh, I 'll be ready faw you,
seh, in ve'y shawt time."

Pink diplomatically steered the young
man over to the window and supplied him
with the remnant of a morning paper, after
which he returned to the morning customer, with a sidewise expression of satis-
fied cunning.

" I do n' wan' no sody-juggleh out o' no
drug-stoah to stan' round an' rubbeh when
I 'm talkin' 'em p'ivate mattchs," he said,
confidentially, as he resumed his place on
the stool. " I got to use him propeh, 'cuz
his money goes on 'e street-cahs jus' same
as yo's, but I sutny do n' want to be con-

f'dential 'ith no boy 'at tosses 'em aig phosphates."

"Well, what's the purport of all this sanguinary conversation?" asked the morning customer, who had noted that Pink always mapped out the vengeance first and told of the provocation afterward.

Pink smiled in upward admiration, and then his shoulders shook in rapid measure, showing that he was enjoying himself inwardly.

"Ev'y day new ones, misteh!" he exclaimed. "Ev'y day new ones! Some hotteh 'an othehs, but all of 'em too wahm faw pooh cullud boy."

"Did n't I understand you to say that you were going to slaughter some one?"

"Misteh, heah's what I'm goin' 'o do: I'm goin' 'o cut my name in 'at cullud rascal so deep 'at you can read it f'om behind same as in front. I'm goin' 'o stand him up an' whittle him. Yes, seh; I'm goin' 'o take off so much o' his

"TOSSES 'EM AIG-PHOSPHATES"

weight 'at he 'll be in new class. I 'll
sutny trim him good. When I finish 'ith
him an' pack my tools, he 'll be diff'ent
shape — 'at 's a fac'."

" I think I begin to understand," said
the morning customer. " Somebody has
stolen that new girl."

" Who? Who? Do n' neveh believe
it, seh. No, seh! If 'ey get 'at lady
'way f'om William Pinckney, 'ey sutny
got to pull 'uh. She could n' leave me if
she want' to. You know what she say?
' Misteh Mahsh, 'ey 's one floweh 'at
blooms in ev'y gahden, an' you ah my
honeysuckle.' "

" That 's very pretty."

" It ain't ev'y dahk-haihed boy 'at gets
'at kind, misteh."

" I suppose not. Well, if you have n't
lost Miss Hopkins, what seems to be the
trouble ? "

" Yes, seh, 'e trouble is, misteh, 'at
some cullud pusson 's out to poison my

cha'cteh. Somebody 's been knockin' me
'ith ol' Mis' Hopkins. Goodness, misteh! She tell Belle 'at she heah I like gin
an' roll 'e bones an' play numbehs an'
cah'y razah, an'—"

"And steal chickens?"

" Suah! Wuhse kind o' chicken-lifteh
—steal 'em in front o' butcheh-shops an'
stoahs—steal 'ese 'at 's picked an' cleaned.
Yes, seh, whoeveh it is 'at 's knockin', I
s'pose, got me down faw stealin' dead
chickens. It takes a spoht to go afteh a
live chicken, misteh, but when you take
dead one, 'at 's jus' plain stealin'. I
s'pose I 'm dead-chicken thief."

" Somebody 's been telling all these
things to Miss Hopkins's mother — is that
it?"

" Misteh, I ought to be oveh in 'e jail,
an' have my pickchah in 'e papeh. Neveh
mind, misteh, I 'm waitin'."

" Do you suspect any one?"

" I 'll tell you 'bout 'at, misteh. Miss

Belle got a cousin, Chesteh Hopkins, 'at leads 'e singin' at e' chuhch. Chesteh got side-whiskehs. Look out faw one 'ith side-whiskehs, mistch! It wuz n' neveh meant faw no cullud pusson to have side-whiskehs. Chesteh got a ve'y wahm set of 'em, too. An' he weahs eyeglasses! Hush! I tell you, mistch, he ain't right. He do n' look like no cullud pusson. He look mo' like some Sunday-school white man 'at jus' shift his cullah. I guess he ain' no cullud man, neetheh, come to think 'bout it. Chesteh wuz 'e fus' Af'o-Ameh'can on Deahbohn Street. He 's suah 'nough Af'o-Ameh'can, an' he got a bad eye in his head faw Misteh William Pinckney Mahsh. Him an' Brotheh Fehguson, 'e preacheh, jus' about own 'at chuhch at ol' Mis' Hopkins goes to, an' I do n' s'pose ol' Chesteh goin' 'o ovehlook no chance to spoil my bets. 'Cose I ain' been goin' to chuhch ve'y often in 'e las' twenty yeahs o' so, an' mebbe Chesteh do n' think I got no ticket faw to swing on 'e sweet cha'iot," and Pink laughed.

"Have n't been to church, and you're proud of it," said the morning customer, shaking his head. "I'm afraid you're a hopeless case."

"I been sev'al times lately 'ith Miss Belle."

"Trying to get on good terms with Mrs. Hopkins."

"I s'pose 'at 's a bad guess, misteh. Anyways I ain't win 'at ol' lady yet. Goodness, misteh! I like to know who feed huh 'at mean talk 'bout me. Somebody scandalize my name, suah. On'y one thing squaih me 'ith Mis' Hopkins—'at 's one of 'em lettehs. Make me good one, misteh, an' put in some sc'ipchah. Ain't scaihed o' losin' my baby, but I want to be so good up at 'e Hopkins house 'at a good wahm dinneh be waitin' faw me any time I call."

The morning customer promised.

"COUSIN CHESTEH"

On Conjuration

The morning customer spent fifteen minutes in composing the letter which was to give Pink Marsh a sure standing with Belle Hopkins's mother. He pushed aside the letters waiting to be answered, and devoted himself to the labor of love. Was he prompted by the hopes of a reward? None—except that reward which comes to the unselfish man when he knows that he has helped to complicate a love affair.

He took it to Mr. Clifford's shop two days after his promise had been given. Pink was anxious to hear the letter, and he exercised great haste in shining a pair of scaly gaiters, so that he could go into a close session with the morning customer.

" Got 'at, misteh ? " he asked, cautiously.

" Which ? O, that letter ? Yes, I dashed off a few lines and had them typewritten. I 've left it so that you can sign your name at the bottom—that is, if it suits you."

" Suit me, misteh ? I know it 's good befo' you read it."

" I did n't know Mrs. Hopkins's first name, so I left that blank. Do you know it ? "

" No, seh, I do n't. Jus' Mis' Hopkins; 'at 's all we eveh call huh."

" Has she got a husband ? "

" Yes, seh, she got a husband."

" What 's his name ? "

" Zig Lucas."

" Her name is Mrs. Hopkins and her husband's name is Zig Lucas—how do you make that out ? "

" Mis' Hopkins, she been mah'ied befo'. I guess so wuz ol' Zig. He got boy

Spotswood Lucas', 'at ain' no kin to Belle at all. Ol' Spot neveh done day's wuhk in his life. Sick all 'e time. Yes, seh, too sick to wuhk—jus' able to eat an' play pool."

" I put it ' Mrs. Hopkins' here. We'll let it go at that. Are you ready to hear it ? "

" Yes, seh, misteh. Do n' make it too loud."

" 'Mrs. Hopkins—My Dear Madam: It is with—' "

" Hold on, misteh. You want to get me in trouble 'ith 'at ol' Zig ? What you got me sayin' to Mis' Hopkins ? "

" Why, you address her as ' My dear madam.' "

" Ain't 'at puhty wahm to give 'at ol' guhl ? When she reads 'at, she think I 'm afteh huh, 'stead o' Belle. ' Deah madam' —my goodness ! 'At 's lovin' talk, suah."

" O, that does n't mean anything. Any letter to a married lady of your acquaint-

ance should begin that way. You leave
it alone. That will please her."

He read the letter:

" MRS. HOPKINS—My Dear Madam: It is
with feelings of indiscriminate respect that I address you upon a subject which I regard as
altogether behooving.

> " ' Be thou as chaste as ice, as pure as snow,
> Thou shalt not escape calumny.'

" How true this is! It is with excruciating
surprise that I learn of a recent attempt to cast
aspersions on my character, which I have always sought to keep herbiverous. As you are
doubtless cognizant, I have lately endeavored
to place myself in immediate juxtaposition to
your daughter, Belle, whose caloric properties
are such as to excite my profound admiration.
At present she is the most salubrious object
within my range of vision. Animated, no
doubt, by the rancor of envy, some inconse-
quential marplot is striving to elucidate my su-
periority. I wish to deny emphatically anything you may hear which is not derogatory to
my character. Without going into details, I
may say with all the vehemence of asseveration,

"BUD"

that I am the most superior Afro-American who ever approached on the rural highway. This epistle will doubtless remove all eccentricities from your mind, and make you disposed to regard me as the proper recipient of gustatory favors. Thanking you for your kind attention, I am, with sufficient respect, yours truly."

While the letter was being read, Pink emitted tremulous groans, and at the conclusion he said, in an awed whisper: "O, man! O, man! O, man!"

"I did n't think it was best to deny, specifically, any of the charges against you," said the morning customer. "I simply put in a general plea and threw you on the mercy of the court. Have you any changes to suggest?"

"Look heah, misteh, why do n't you ask me to go out an' change 'e stahs in 'e sky? No, seh; 'at lettch 's too good faw any boy my ej'cation to trifle 'ith it. When Mis' Hopkins read 'at, she 'll know I 'm good.

I can jus' see myse'f eatin' Sunday dinneh up at 'at house."

" You 've never eaten up there yet, eh?"

" I do n' daih to, misteh; no, seh."

" Why not? "

" I 'm 'fraid of 'at ol' guhl. She 's f'om Kentucky, an' she knows too much. I 'm 'fraid she 'd cunjuh me, suah."

" Conjure you? What does that mean? "

" Hush, misteh, you know what 'at means betteh 'an I do — a man yo' ej'ca-tion."

" I assure you that I do n't know. How could Mrs. Hopkins conjure you? "

" Well, misteh, I do n' hahdly b'lieve it myse'f, but I heah them Southehn cullud people tell 'bout puttin' 'at stuff in yo' eatin', an' it make someping grow inside o' you — someping like lizahd."

" O, pshaw! You do n't believe all that stuff, do you? "

" Look heah, misteh man, some of 'em

ol' cullud people 'at's lived down South can use you bad if you ain' caihful. Bud Law'ence tol' me he saw man in Kentucky 'at got cunjuhed by an ol' cullud lady, an' he had to sen' to Loueyville faw ol' cullud doctah. Doctah come an' dig all 'em roots an' 'uhbs an' make tea faw 'at cullud man, an' he toss up two white lizahds. 'At's what Bud seen 'ith his own eyes."

" How did these lizards get into him? "

" My goodness! He got cunjuhed, misteh — at's how he got 'em. He had fuss 'ith an ol' cullud lady, an' she put 'at cunjuh stuff in his dinneh. Yes, seh, you can laugh, misteh, but 'ey's sutny someping in 'at cunjuh business. Look heah, seh, did n' you eveh put hoss-haih into bottle an' see it tuhn into snake? Yes, seh, I seen 'at myse'f. 'At's what 'em cunjuh people do — put someping like 'at into yo' victuals, an' it get inside o' you, an' you begin feelin' bad an' get thinneh an' thinneh, an' if you do n' get 'at boy out o' you

—goin' 'o have a black beh'yin, suah.
Yes, seh, 'em cunjuh people come an' plant
someping in front o' yo' house, too. You
walk oveh it ev'y day, an' afteh while you
get sick, an' fus' thing you know you jus'
tuhn up yo' toes. I do n' want nothin' to
do 'ith 'em cunjuh people."

"Well, do you think Mrs. Hopkins has
the power to conjure you?"

"Yes, seh, most any o' 'em ol' cullud
ladies f'om 'e South got 'at poweh. Ol'
Pink sutny ain' goin' 'o eat no dinneh in
'at house 'til he knows 'at Mis' Hopkins
likes him. She's been talkin' bad 'bout
me, an' I go to 'at house an' eat — you
do n' know what she do to me!"

"Have n't you got your rabbit's foot?"

"Yes, seh, you can laugh, misteh, but
do n't you fool yo'se'f 'bout 'at cunjuh'n.
Someping in it, suah."

Pink shook his head solemnly, and appeared to be somewhat grieved that the
morning customer went away laughing.

"TOO SICK TO WUHK"

On the Doubts which Precede Matrimony

Pink Marsh reported to the morning customer that the letter to Mrs. Hopkins had accomplished its purpose.

"She ain't th'ough lookin' oveh 'at letteh yet," he said, shaking his head and bubbling with laughter. " Ol' Zig, he did n' eveh b'lieve I wrote it. He tell Belle to ask me who wrote 'at letteh. I say, ' Look it oveh, guhl, an' see whose name 's down at 'e bottom.' My goodness, misteh! 'At letteh did suit ol' Mis' Hopkins! She likes 'em hot wuhds, just 'e kind you put in 'at letteh. Yes, seh, when Brotheh Fehguson up at 'e chuhch begin to toss 'em hot wuhds at 'e brethe'n an' sistuhn, 'at 's when ol' Mis' Hopkins begin to get happy an' let go."

" You do n't think she 'll conjure you now?"

" Cunjuh me, misteh? Pink is huh honey-boy now—suah! She likes me now,'cuz she find out I got wahm ej'cation. All 'at talk 'bout 'medimate justamisition—"

" ' Immediate juxtaposition' ?"

" Yes, seh; 'at 's what win ol' Mis' Hopkins. She 's sutny usin' me good 'ese days. ' Misteh Mahsh, I hope yo' feelin' ambulous 'iss ev'nin'. ' O yes, Mis' Hopkins, I 'm ve'y lansimous."

" You did n't tell her you were lansimous, did you ? "

" W'y — yes seh. I jus' say like 'at, ' I'm feelin' ratheh lansimous.' "

" ' Lansimous' means that you are suffering from remorse — that you 've got something on your mind."

" Yes, seh; 'at 's so, misteh; but Mis' Hopkins she did n' know what 'at meant. I s'pose she thought I jus' meant I wuz feelin' well."

"OL' ZIG"

" So you 're welcome to the house now ? "

" Hush, man ! Las' night an' night befo'. Settin' on 'e front steps 'ith my sweet thing, an' holdin' on to huh so she would n' get lost. O, I guess she 's pooh," and Pink hit the box with his polishing-brush and laughed immoderately.

" Well, if Mrs. Hopkins is won over and Belle loves you, I do n't see that there is anything to prevent an early union."

" You mean faw us to get mah'ied ? "

" Why, certainly. You 've been court-ing this girl for several weeks, have n't you ? You say she loves you, and, accord-ing to your own admission, you have visited her at her home and sat on the front steps with her — probably embraced her."

Pink was bent over the shoe, quivering with laughter at the recital.

" I have helped you to win the favor of the young lady's mother," continued the morning customer. "Now that the girl and her mother trust you, are you going to betray that trust? You talk as if you did n't intend to marry her at all."

"Look heah, misteh," said Pink, still bubbling with laughter, "what you think we goin' 'o live on — buck dances? In 'e fus' place, 'at maih'age license cost two dollahs. I ain't even got nasty ol' two, no, seh! How 'bout 'em lace cuhtains faw windows, an' pohk-chops to eat ev'y mawnin'? Huh-uh! Can 't get mah'ied till I got 'at roll."

"About the first time I ever came into this shop, six months ago, I advised you to begin saving your money. If you had started in and saved two dollars a week, you would have had fifty or sixty dollars by this time. With that much you could have bought a new suit of clothes, rented a house and made a first payment on some furniture. As it is, how much have you this morning?"

"DRIVES CAIH'AGE"

" Mistch, if 'ey had n't rung in hosses on me las' night, I 'd have sev'al dollahs 'iss mawnin'."

" So you 've been playing craps again ? That was after your call on Miss Hopkins, I presume."

" Yes, seh; I had 'em comin' good, but little Joe use me bad, an' somebody get in hosses, an' 'en a big cullud fellow 'at drives caih'age jus' took me 'way in his cloze. Ol' Gawge Lippincott went broke, too."

" Well, there you are again — gambling? Does this girl know that you gamble ? "

" She do n' caih how much I gamble, if I on'y pull out someping. Co'se she got no use faw man 'at 's cleaned all 'e time. You got to flash two-bit piece once in awhile to keep 'em smilin'."

" Well, what will be the outcome of this affair with Miss Hopkins? If you do n't intend to marry her, why have you pursued her?"

"Look heah, misteh, I do n' say I won't mah'y 'at Miss Belle Hopkins. I s'pose I might if I had mo' money; but you know what I say to you heah one day — cake-walks is good, but you sutny can't eat 'em. If I jus' get on good live one some time, 'bout fawty to one, an' play five dollahs — hush, misteh! We be livin' in one of 'em white houses 'ith blue cuh-tains in 'e windows, an' all 'em red velvet sofys an' chaihs, wall-papeh covehed 'ith mawnin'-glo'ies, Brussel cahpet on 'e flooh—"

"Picture of Peter Jackson in the par-lor," suggested the morning customer.

Pink yawped at the idea, and leaned forward on the box in a convulsion of mirth.

"Misteh, yo' sutny good! Yes, seh; we got to have ol' Peteh. My goodness! 'At 's fine house I got, suah! I can jus'

see myse'f settin' in 'at house eatin'
chicken 'ith home gravy — betteh'n any
of 'iss heah rest'ant gravy, too! Home
gravy an' sweet potatoes! My goodness!
I jus' lingeh 'round 'e table an' make
trouble faw 'at kind o' eatin', I s'pose. I
guess I jus' hate 'at home gravy. Um-
m-m-m! It's ba-a-d!"

By this time Pink was talking to himself and wagging his head gravely. The
morning customer interrupted the solil-
oquy, and said "I'm afraid you'll never
realize your expectations, unless you stop
playing craps."

"Some day I'll get 'em goin', an' I'll
have all 'e money on 'e South Side. Yes,
seh; 'Keep on a-tryin', brotheh,' 'at's jus'
what Preacheh Fehguson says. You'll
see, misteh. I jus' feel 'at I got money
comin' to me."

The morning customer went away, leaving Pink cheered and uplifted by the abid-
ing pleasures of hope.

On Doing the Best One Can

" He come in here yesterday smokin' a big cigar and all dressed up in his best clothes, and said he 'd quit — said he had something better."

Mr. Clifford was speaking. The morning customer stood in hesitancy, looking at the half-grown colored youth who sat on Pink's stool in the corner, humped above a patent-leather shoe which had the shape of a sword-fish.

" You do n't know where he went ? " asked the morning customer.

" No, and I do n't care. I won't have him around here again. This new boy 's all right. He 'll give you a good shine."

Mr. Clifford evidently believed that the morning customer had been coming into the place to have his shoes shined!

The morning customer murmured a falsehood to the effect that he might " come in later," and then he retreated, before Mr. Clifford could say anything more in favor of the new boy.

That was his last visit to the shop. He rather expected to receive a communication from Pink, but no postal-card came, and, to tell the truth, after a few days had passed, he gave no further thought to the " lansimous " boy and his quest for a " baby."

In a busy town, such as Chicago, experiences crowd upon one another, and every live man of the morning-customer kind is so intent on making his fortune that he has little time to tilt back and wonder what has become of the friends of yesterday. Within a month after the disappearance, the season of helpful talks with Pink became ancient history. The morning customer hurried past Mr. Clifford's shop day after day, without seeing it or knowing of its existence. He would be whispering to himself the terms of a contract, or squinting through his glasses to see into the plans of those who wanted to keep him away from his fortune. To such a man, buildings fuse into one another as they slide by in panorama, and pedestrians are so many things to be dodged. The morning customer raced every day. He went to a " parlor " to have his shoes cleaned. Twelve white boys in blue jackets leaned over in a row and worked at high speed. They seldom spoke to the men in the chairs, who regarded one another with fretful suspicion, and turned their morning papers over and over and inside out.

It would be satisfying to know that the morning customer often smiled at recollection of what Pink had told him, and wondered if the boy had saved any money.

He had not the time. That is the fact of the matter. He was jumping with elevators, a hundred feet at an upward leap; racing to court-rooms, where he messed papers and whispered with hollow-eyed accomplices; and sometimes he went out of town on night trains, so as to avoid the deadly sin of traveling during business hours.

One night he boarded a train at a sub-urban crossing. The train was bound for Kansas City. In the sleeping-car the berths were " made up." He went along the narrow aisle between the stuffy cur-tains to where a porter with a white coat was whispering to some hidden passenger. He nudged the porter from behind.

" My goodness, mistch ! "

It was Pink.

" Any lowers left ? " asked the morning customer, closing his teeth together in the endeavor to keep a serious face.

" Well, my goodness, misteh ! Well, seh, it 's you, suah ! My goodness ! I 'm sutny glad to see you once mo'. I declaih!"

"I did n't expect to see *you*, Pink. Have you a lower berth."

"Misteh, if I did n' have none, I'd jus' tuhn somebody out an' let you have it. My goodness! Well! Well!"

"Where 's the conductor."

"Yes, seh, he 's in 'e cah ahead, seh."

"Well, I'll sit in the smoking-room a while."

He went into the smoking compartment and lighted a cigar. A short man with jewelry and a silk cap had been holding the compartment alone. He looked up, as if in annoyance, when the morning customer came in, and then threw away his cigar and rocked away to bed.

The morning customer sprawled out on the plush cushion and smoked. He grinned around his cigar, and once or twice he laughed aloud. Presently Pink slipped in and sat on a low stool. He looked steadfastly at the morning customer

FANNIE

for many seconds, his eyes rolled sidewise, and then he burst into laughter.

" Well, my goodness ! " he said.

" You 're a real porter, now."

" Me an' Misteh Pullman's 'e real boys, suah. No mo' settin' round 'ith 'em white bahbehs. Huh-uh ! "

He paused and looked at the morning customer in blissful silence, and then gave another bellow of laughter, so that he had to restrain himself by putting one hand over his mouth.

" What 's the matter with you, any-way ? " asked the morning customer, leaning forward so as to make himself heard above the pounding of the train.

" Misteh, someping happen to me since I seen you."

" What was it ? "

" Make a guess, misteh," and he was still laughing.

" I know, all right. Did you go and do it ? "

" Look out, misteh! Do n't ask! Ol'
Misteh Mahsh mah'ied man."

The morning customer smiled benevo-
lently. "Glad to hear it," said he.
"What was her name — Belle?"

"Who? 'At Belle Hopkins? No,
seh! Huh-uh! I did n' mah'y 'at guhl."

"You did n't?"

"Look heah, misteh! Crep' up to 'at
house one night an' ketch new cullud boy
'ith both ahms 'round 'at guhl. I jus' say,
'Good-by, my honey!' Yes, seh, she
lose Misteh Mahsh. Got someping betteh
'n 'at Belle. Got lady 'at had p'opehty.
Go 'way! I s'pose I do n' know thing!"

"Got property, eh?"

"Yes, seh — widow."

"A widow!"

"No mo' room-rents, misteh. I jus'
look oveh 'at Mis' White's house an' say,
'O, I guess 'iss 'll do me.' I had huh
lovin' me befo' she know me two days. I
went faw 'at lady an' I landed 'uh."

" How long have you been married? "

" Mo' 'an a month."

" Is she a young woman? "

" She ain't young as some of 'em otheh babies I had lookin' out faw me, but you 'membeh what I tol' you once, misteh? Cake-walks is good, but you can 't eat 'em. You do n' ketch me stahvin'.   No, seh! 'At lady I got ain't so wahm on cloze as some of 'em, but she sutny fix up a pohk chop 'at 's bad to eat.   'At love 's all right, misteh; but Misteh Mahsh sutny got to have his pohk chops."

" Well, are you saving any money? "

" Look heah!   Fannie takes 'at money 'way f'om me an' jus' gives me 'nough to live on.   My goodness, misteh!   I sutny got to hold out on Fannie when I play 'em numbehs."

" Have you caught anything yet? "

" No, seh; but I come might' neah it las' week.   Got two of 'em — want fawty-eight, an' fawty-sevem come."

" What became of the other girl —
Belle? "

" Do n' ask me, misteh! She 's nothin'
to me — no, seh. Huh an' 'at Lo'ena
Jackson — look heah! I 'll have one of
'em guhls hiahed to wuhk 'round 'e house
an' help Fannie."

" I thought you were going to marry
Belle."

" No, seh, I neveh caih faw 'at guhl noways. I done betteh! My goodness,
misteh! I s'pose I 'm pooh. Got my own
dooh-step to set on, new suit o' cloze,
joined 'e lodge. Do n' speak to 'em cheap
cullud people no mo'. Goin' 'o tuhn in,
seh? Jus' you put 'em shoes outside an'
I 'll give 'em one of 'em ol' shines like
you use' to get."

The morning customer rolled into a
lower berth, and lay between the cool
sheets, smiling hard at the upper berth,
which Pink had lifted out of the way, in
violation of a very strict rule. The morn-

ing customer paid for a lower berth, and owned a section. He was trying to imagine Pink's house — the wall-paper, the illuminated curtains, the nickeled stove in the front room, and the picture of Abraham Lincoln. He heard creeping footfalls just outside his berth, and then a voice, " Good-night, seh."

PRINTED AT THE LAKESIDE PRESS
FOR HERBERT S. STONE & CO.
PUBLISHERS, CHICAGO

By the author of "**PINK MARSH**"

ARTIE : A Story of the Streets and Town.

By GEORGE ADE. With many illustrations by
John T. McCutcheon. 16mo, $1.25

_____

Ninth thousand.

"Mr. Ade shows all the qualities of a successful novelist."— *Chicago Tribune.*

"Artie is a character, and George Ade has limned
him deftly, as well as amusingly. Under his rollicking
abandon and recklessness we are made to feel the real
sense and sensitiveness and the worldly wisdom of a
youth whose only language is that of a street-gamin.
As a study of the peculiar type chosen, it is both typical
and inimitable."— *Detroit Free Press.*

"It is brimful of fun and picturesque slang. Nobody
will be any the worse for reading about Artie. If he does
talk slang. He 's a good fellow at heart, and Mamie
Carroll is the ' making of him.' He talks good sense and
good morality, and these things haven't yet gone out
of style, even in Chicago."— *New York Recorder.*

"Well-meaning admirers have compared Artie to
Chimmie Fadden, but Mr. Townsend's creation, excellent
as it is, cannot be said to be entirely free from exaggeration. The hand of Chimmie Fadden's maker is to be
discerned at times. And just here Artie is particularly
strong — he is always Artie, and Mr. Ade is always concealed, and never obtrudes his personality."— *Chicago
Post.*

"George Ade is a writer, the direct antithesis of
Stephen Crane. In 'Artie' he has given the world a story
of the streets at once wholesome, free, and stimulating.
The world is filled with people like 'Artie' Blanchard
and his 'girl,' 'Mamie' Carroll, and the story of their lives,
their hopes, and dreams, and loves, is immeasurably
more wholesome than all the stories like 'George's Mother' that could be written by an army of the writers who
call themselves realists."— Editorial, *Albany Evening
Journal.*

To be had of all booksellers, or will be sent, post-paid, on
receipt of price by the Publishers.

CATALOGUE · OF · BOOKS · IN · BELLES · LETTRES

Chicago   New York

MDCCCXCVII

MESSRS. HERBERT S. STONE & COMPANY TAKE PLEASURE IN ANNOUNCING THE FOLLOWING PUBLICATIONS AS IN PREPARATION:

The next novel by Harold Frederic,
Author of "The Damnation of Theron Ware."

" Dross," a novel by Henry Seton Merriman.
Author of " The Sowers," etc.

And new books by George Ade, author of " Artie," and Henry M. Blossom, Jr., Author of "Checkers."

Further particulars will be given later.

LONDON OFFICE: 10 NORFOLK ST., STRAND.
CABLE ADDRESSES:
" CHAPBOOK, CHICAGO."
" CHAPBOOK, NEW YORK."
" EDITORSHIP, LONDON."

THE PUBLICATIONS OF HERBERT S. STONE & CO. THE CHAP-BOOK

CAXTON BUILDING, CHICAGO
111 FIFTH AVENUE, NEW YORK

Ade, George.
ARTIE: *A Story of the Streets and of the Town. With many pictures by* JOHN T. McCUTCHEON. *16mo. $1.25.*

Ninth thousand.

" Mr. Ade shows all the qualities of a successful novelist."—*Chicago Tribune.*

" Artie is a character, and George Ade has limned him deftly as well as amusingly. Under his rollicking abandon and recklessness we are made to feel the real sense and sensitiveness, and the worldly wisdom of a youth whose only language is that of a street-gamin. As a study of the peculiar type chosen, it is both typical and inimitable."—*Detroit Free Press.*

" It is brimful of fun and picturesque slang. Nobody will be any the worse for reading about Artie, if he does talk slang. He 's a good fellow at heart, and Mamie Carroll is the 'making of him.' He talks good sense and good morality, and these things have n't yet gone out of style, even in Chicago."—*New York Recorder.*

" Well-meaning admirers have compared Artie

3

to Chimmie Fadden, but Mr. Townsend's creation, excellent as it is, cannot be said to be entirely free from exaggeration. The hand of Chimmie Fadden's maker is to be discerned at times. And just here Artie is particularly strong—he is always Artie, and Mr. Ade is always concealed, and never obtrudes his personality."—*Chicago Post.*

"George Ade is a writer, the direct antithesis of Stephen Crane. In 'Artie' he has given the world a story of the streets at once wholesome, free, and stimulating. The world is filled with people like 'Artie' Blanchard and his 'girl,' 'Mamie' Carroll, and the story of their lives, their hopes, and dreams, and loves, is immeasurably more wholesome than all the stories like 'George's Mother' that could be written by an army of the writers who call themselves realists."—Editorial *Albany Evening Journal.*

Benham, Charles.
THE FOURTH NAPOLEON: *A Romance.*
12mo. $1.50.

An accurate account of the history of the Fourth Napoleon, the *coup d'état* which places him on the throne of France, the war with Germany, and his love intrigues as emperor. A vivid picture of contemporary politics in Paris.

Blossom, Henry M., Jr.
CHECKERS: *A Hard-Luck Story. By the author of* "*The Documents in Evidence.*" *16mo.* $1.25. *Seventh edition.*

"Abounds in the most racy and picturesque slang."—*New York Recorder.*

"'Checkers' is an interesting and entertaining

chap, a distinct type, with a separate tongue and a way of saying things that is oddly humorous."— *Chicago Record.*

"If I had to ride from New York to Chicago on a slow train, I should like a half-dozen books as gladsome as 'Checkers,' and I could laugh at the trip."—*New York Commercial Advertiser.*

"'Checkers' himself is as distinct a creation as Chimmie Fadden, and his racy slang expresses a livelier wit. The racing part is clever reporting, and as horsey and 'up to date' as any one could ask. The slang of the racecourse is caught with skill and is vivid and picturesque, and students of the byways of language may find some new gems of colloquial speech to add to their lexicons."— *Springfield Republican.*

Chap-Book Essays.

A VOLUME OF REPRINTS FROM THE CHAP-BOOK. *Contributions by* T. W. HIGGINSON, H. W. MABIE, LOUISE CHANDLER MOULTON, H. H. BOYE-SEN, EDMUND GOSSE, JOHN BURROUGHS, NORMAN HAPGOOD, MRS. REGINALD DE KOVEN, LOUISE IMOGEN GUINEY, LEWIS E. GATES, ALICE MORSE EARLE, LAURENCE JERROLD, RICHARD HENRY STODDARD, EVE BLANTYRE SIMPSON, *and* MAURICE THOMPSON, *with a cover designed by* A. E. BORIE. *16mo.* $1.25.

Chap-Book Stories.

A VOLUME OF REPRINTS FROM THE CHAP-BOOK. *Contributions by* OCTAVE THANET, GRACE ELLERY CHANNING, MARIA LOUISE POOL, *and Others. 16mo.* $1.25. *Second edition.*

The authors of this volume are all American. Besides the well-known names, there are some which were seen in the CHAP-BOOK for the first time. The volume is bound in an entirely new and startling fashion.

Chatfield-Taylor, H. C.

THE LAND OF THE CASTANET: *Spanish Sketches, with twenty-five full-page illustrations. 12mo.* $1.25.

"Gives the reader an insight into the life of Spain at the present time which he cannot get elsewhere."—*Cincinnati Commercial Tribune.*

"Mr. Chatfield-Taylor's word-painting of special events—the bull-fight, for instance—is vivid and well-colored. He gets at the national character very well indeed, and we feel that we know our Spain better by reason of his handsome little book."—*Boston Traveler.*

"He writes pleasantly and impartially, and very fairly sums up the Spanish character. . . . Mr. Taylor's book is well illustrated, and is more readable than the reminiscences of the average globetrotter."—*New York Sun.*

D'Annunzio, Gabriele.

EPISCOPO AND COMPANY. *Translated by Myrta Leonora Jones. 16mo. $1.25.*
Second edition.

Gabriele d'Annunzio is the best-known and most gifted of modern Italian novelists. His work is making a great sensation at present in all literary circles. The translation now offered gives the first opportunity English-speaking readers have had to know him in their own language.

De Fontenoy, The Marquise.

EVE'S GLOSSARY. *By the author of "Queer Sprigs of Gentility," with decorations in two colors by* FRANK HAZENPLUG. *4to.*
Nearly ready.

An amusing volume of gossip and advice for gentlewomen. It treats of health, costume, and entertainments; exemplifies by reference to noted beauties of England and the Continent; and is embellished with decorative borders of great charm.

Earle, Alice Morse.

CURIOUS PUNISHMENTS OF BYGONE DAYS, *with twelve quaint pictures and a cover design by* FRANK HAZENPLUG. *12mo. $1.50.*

"In this dainty little volume, Alice Morse Earle has done a real service, not only to present readers, but to future students of bygone customs. To come upon all the information that is here put into readable shape, one would be obliged to search

7

through many ancient and cumbrous records."—
Boston Transcript.

"Mrs. Alice Morse Earle has made a diverting and edifying book in her 'Curious Punishments of Bygone Days,' which is published in a style of quaintness befitting the theme."—*New York Tribune*

"This light and entertaining volume is the most recent of Mrs. Earle's popular antiquarian sketches, and will not fail to amuse and mildly instruct readers who love to recall the grim furnishings and habits of previous centuries, without too much serious consideration of the root from which they sprang, the circumstances in which they flourished, or the uses they served."—*The Independent.*

Hichens, Robert.

FLAMES : *A novel. By the author of "A Green Carnation," "An Imaginative Man," "The Folly of Eustace," etc., with a cover-design by* F. R. KIMBROUGH. *12mo. $1.50.*

Mr. Hichens's reputation has steadily increased since the brilliant success of "A Green Carnation" first gave him prominence. His latest work is longer and more important than anything he has done before.

James, Henry.

WHAT MAISIE KNEW: *A novel. 12mo.* (*In preparation.*)

Upon its completion in the CHAP-BOOK, Mr. Henry James's latest novel will be issued in book-form. Its publication cannot fail to be an event of no slight literary importance, and will be worthy the attention of all persons interested in English and American letters.

Kinross, Albert.

THE FEARSOME ISLAND ; *Being a modern rendering of the narrative of one Silas Fordred, Master Mariner of Hythe, whose shipwreck and subsequent adventures are herein set forth. Also an appendix, accounting in a rational manner for the seeming marvels that Silas Fordred encountered during his sojourn on the fearsome island of Don Diego Rodriguez. With a cover designed by* FRANK HAZENPLUG. *16mo.* $1.25.

Le Gallienne, Richard.

PROSE FANCIES: *Second series. By the author of "The Book-Bills of Narcissus," "The Quest of the Golden Girl," etc. With a cover designed by* FRANK HAZENPLUG. *16mo.* $12.5. *Second edition.*

" In these days of Beardsley pictures and decadent novels, it is good to find a book as sweet, as pure, as delicate as Mr. Le Gallienne's."—*New Orleans Picayune.*

"'Prose Fancies' ought to be in every one's summer library, for it is just the kind of a book one loves to take to some secluded spot to read and dream over."—*Kansas City Times.*

" There are witty bits of sayings by the score,
and sometimes whole paragraphs of nothing but
wit. Somewhere there is a little skit about 'Scot-
land, the country that takes its name from the
whisky made there'; and the transposed proverbs,
like 'It is an ill wind for the shorn lamb,' and
'Many rise on the stepping-stones of their dead
relations,' are brilliant. 'Most of us would never
be heard of were it not for our enemies,' is a cap-
ital epigram."—*Chicago Times-Herald.*

"Mr. Le Gallienne is first of all a poet, and these
little essays, which savor somewhat of Lamb, of
Montaigne, of Lang, and of Birrell, are larded
with verse of exquisite grace. He rarely ventures
into the grotesque, but his fancy follows fair
paths; a certain quaintness of expression and the
idyllic atmosphere of the book charm one at the
beginning and carry one through the nineteen
'fancies' that comprise the volume."—*Chicago
Record.*

Magruder, Julia.

Miss Ayr of Virginia, and Other
Stories. *By the author of "The Princess
Sonia," "The Violet," etc. With a
cover-design by* F. R. Kimbrough. *16mo.
$1.25.*

" By means of original incident and keen portraiture, 'Miss Ayr of Virginia, and Other Stories,'
is made a decidedly readable collection. In the
initial tale the character of the young Southern
girl is especially well drawn; Miss Magruder's
most artistic work, however, is found at the end
of the volume, under the title 'Once More.'"—*The
Outlook.*

"The contents of ' Miss Ayr of Virginia' are not

less fascinating than the cover. . . . These tales . . . are a delightful diversion for a spare hour. They are dreamy without being candidly realistic, and are absolutely refreshing in the simplicity of the author's style."—*Boston Herald.*

"Julia Magruder's stories are so good that one feels like reading passages here and there again and again. In the collection, 'Miss Ayr of Virginia, and Other Stories,' she is at her best, and 'Miss Ayr of Virginia,' has all the daintiness, the point and pith and charm which the author so well commands. The portraiture of a sweet, unsophisticated, pretty, smart Southern girl is bewitching."—*Minneapolis Times.*

Malet, Lucas.

THE CARISSIMA: *A modern grotesque. By the author of " The Wages of Sin," etc. 12mo. $1.50. Second edition.*

*** This is the first novel which Lucas Malet has written since "The Wages of Sin."

"The strongest piece of fiction written during the year, barring only the masters, Meredith and Thomas Hardy."—*Kansas City Star.*

"There are no dull pages in " The Carissima," no perfunctory people. Every character that goes in and out on the mimic stage is fully rounded, and the central one provokes curiosity, like those of that Sphinx among novelists, Mr. Henry James. Lucas Malet has caught the very trick of James's manner, and the likeness presses more than once."—*Milwaukee Sentinel.*

"The interest throughout the story is intense and perfectly sustained. The character-drawing is as good as it can be. The Carissima, her father, and a journalistic admirer are, in particular, absolute triumphs. The book is wonderfully witty, and has touches of genuine pathos, more than two and more than three. It is much better than anything else we have seen from the same hand."—*Pall Mall Gazette.*

"Lucas Malet has insight, strength, the gift of satire, and a captivating brilliance of touch; in short, a literary equipment such as not too many present-day novelists are possessed of."—*London Daily Mail.*

"We cannot think of readers as skipping a line or failing to admire the workmanship, or to be deeply interested, both in the characters and the plot. 'Carissima' is likely to add to the reputation of the author of ' The Wages of Sin.'"—*Glasgow Herald.*

Moore, F. Frankfort.
THE IMPUDENT COMEDIAN AND OTHERS. *Illustrated. 12mo. $1.50.*

Several of the stories have appeared in the CHAP-BOOK; others are now published for the first time. They all relate to seventeenth and eighteenth century characters—Nell Gwynn, Kitty Clive, Oliver Goldsmith, Dr. Johnson, and David Garrick. They are bright, witty, and dramatic.

THE JESSAMY BRIDE: *A Novel. By the author of "The Impudent Comedian." 12mo. $1.50.*

A novel of great interest, introducing as its chief characters Goldsmith, Johnson, Garrick, Sir Joshua Reynolds and others. It is really a companion volume to "The Impudent Comedian."

Morrison, Arthur.

A CHILD OF THE JAGO. *By the author of "Tales of Mean Streets." 12mo. $1.50. Second edition.*

***This, the first long story which Mr. Morrison has written, is, like his remarkable "Tales of Mean Streets," a realistic study of East End life.

"The power and art of the book are beyond question."—*Hartford Courant.*

"It is one of the most notable books of the year."—*Chicago Daily News.*

"'A Child of the Jago' will prove one of the immediate and great successes of the season."—*Boston Times.*

"Since Daniel Defoe, no such consummate master of realistic fiction has arisen among us as Mr. Arthur Morrison. Hardly any praise could be too much for the imaginative power and artistic perfection and beauty of this picture of the depraved and loathsome phases of human life. There is all of Defoe's fidelity of realistic detail, suffused with the light and warmth of a genius higher and purer than Defoe's."—*Scotsman.*

"It more than fulfills the promise of 'Tales of Mean Streets'—it makes you confident that Mr. Morrison has yet better work to do. The power displayed is magnificent, and the episode of the murder of Weech, 'fence' and 'nark,' and of the capture and trial of his murderer, is one that stamps itself upon the memory as a thing done once and for all. Perrott in the dock, or as he awaits the executioner, is a fit companion of Fagin condemned. The book cannot but confirm the admirers of Mr. Morrison's remarkable talent in the opinions they formed on reading 'Tales of Mean Streets.'"—*Black and White.*

"Mr. Morrison has achieved an astonishing success. Take it as a whole, as a picture of a phase of life, and you must admit that it is a masterly achievement—a triumph of art. It is a distinct advance upon his earlier book, 'Tales of Mean Streets,' because, it seems to us, it is truer, more convincing, less dispiriting. The biggest thing in the book is the description of him after the murder, and when he is on trial. It is a wonderful bit of psychology; done so simply, and apparently without any eye to effect, but overpoweringly convincing. The book is a masterpiece."—*Pall Mall Gazette.*

Pool, Maria Louise.

IN BUNCOMBE COUNTY. *16mo.* $1.25.
Second edition.

"'In Buncombe County' is bubbling over with merriment—one could not be blue with such a companion for an hour."—*Boston Times.*

"Maria Louise Pool is a joy forever, principally because she so nobly disproves the lurking theory that women are born destitute of humor. Hers is not acquired; it is the real thing. 'In Buncombe County' is perfect with its quiet appreciation of the humorous side of the every-day affairs of life."—*Chicago Daily News.*

"It is brimming over with humor, and the reader who can follow the fortunes of the redbird alone, who flutters through the first few chapters, and not be moved to long laughter, must be sadly insensitive. But laugh as he may, he will always revert to the graver vein which unobtrusively runs from the first to the last page in the book. He will lay down the narrative of almost grotesque adventure with a keen remembrance of its tenderness and pathos."—*New York Tribune.*

Pritchard, Martin J.

WITHOUT SIN: *A novel. 12mo. $1.50.*
Third edition.

*₊*The New York *Journal* gave a half-page review of the book and proclaimed it "the most startling novel yet."

"Abounds in situations of thrilling interest. A unique and daring book."—*Review of Reviews* (London).

"One is hardly likely to go far wrong in predicting that 'Without Sin' will attract abundant notice. Too much can scarcely be said in praise of Mr. Pritchard's treatment of his subject."—*Academy.*

"The very ingenious way in which improbable incidents are made to appear natural, the ingenious manner in which the story is sustained to the end, the undoubted fascination of the writing, and the convincing charm of the principal characters, are just what make this novel so deeply dangerous while so intensely interesting."—*The World* (London).

Raimond, C. E.

THE FATAL GIFT OF BEAUTY, AND OTHER STORIES. *By the Author of* "*George Mandeville's Husband,*" *etc. 16mo. $1.25.*

A book of stories which will not quickly be surpassed for real humor, skillful characterization and splendid entertainment. "The Confessions of a Cruel Mistress" is a masterpiece, and the "Portman Memoirs" are exceptionally clever.

FAIRE ET TAIRE